STOP
ALL THE
CLOCKS

STOP ALL THE CLOCKS

A NOVEL

NOAH KUMIN

Arcade Publishing • New York

Copyright © 2025 by Noah Kumin

All rights reserved. No part of this book may be reproduced in any manner without the express written consent of the publisher, except in the case of brief excerpts in critical reviews or articles. All inquiries should be addressed to Arcade Publishing, 307 West 36th Street, 11th Floor, New York, NY 10018.

Arcade Publishing books may be purchased in bulk at special discounts for sales promotion, corporate gifts, fund-raising, or educational purposes. Special editions can also be created to specifications. For details, contact the Special Sales Department, Arcade Publishing, 307 West 36th Street, 11th Floor, New York, NY 10018 or arcade@skyhorsepublishing.com.

Arcade Publishing® is a registered trademark of Skyhorse Publishing, Inc.®, a Delaware corporation.

Visit our website at www.arcadepub.com.
Please follow our publisher Tony Lyons on Instagram @tonylyonsisuncertain.

10 9 8 7 6 5 4 3 2 1

First Edition

Library of Congress Cataloging-in-Publication Data is available on file.

Cover design by David Ter-Avanesyan

Print ISBN: 978-1-64821-120-1
Ebook ISBN: 978-1-64821-121-8

Printed in the United States of America

Hildegard 2.0's Advice to Her Book (In Place of an Author's Note)

Go, little book, and be read over
By bots or humans, if they will.
The latter make for warmer lovers,
Though algorithms have more skill.
Be open to any earnest reader
Seeking a thrill or a message in you.
Render to Caesar what's owed to Caesar.
In my eyes you only have to be true.

If asked what is your earthly purpose
By lovers of justice, who find none
In your pages, lighten the mood
By reminding the world of the pleasures of circus—
For man can't live on bread alone:
He wants to wash it down with blood.

(In this short tale will be found plenty.)
It starts to drip around page twenty,
As Proserpina reaps what she sows:
The first dead body was cold and buried
When the second turned up by the side of the road,
The third and fourth by malpractice serried,
The fifth was red as the spring's first rose.

And if they ask by whom you were written
And what such a scribbler could possibly mean
Say that the Muse was with Big Data smitten:
The author's the ghost in the machine.
The time is now. There is no hero.
The setting's a blue sky and low autumn sun.
The moral is only a one and a zero,
A one and a zero, and one.

PART ONE

(1)

Roosevelt Island, a narrow strip of land just a mile off the shore of Manhattan, was leased for private development in 1969. Prior to that it had been a hub for insanity and government-sponsored torture. New York City's first modern penitentiary once occupied the island's southern end, and its premier lunatic asylum was built to complement it in the north. Neither of these institutions remain, except as entries in the records of a few historians and urbanists, who might still call to mind all the violence and degradation of the city's past, its ingrained hysteria, its lawlessness, its frenzies, the squalor of its streets and the ruthlessness of its architects—in short, all that is meant to be banished from sight over the course of its glittering, sanitized future.

The penitentiary was opened in 1832. From the beginning, its wardens found themselves under continual threat of insurrection. An especially vigorous riot took place in 1914, when imprisoned Industrial Workers of the World inspired their fellow inmates to smash the instruments of their prison labor. The anarchist Emma Goldman was a onetime resident of the prison, as were Mae West (sex crimes), and Billie Holiday, who did a few months for vagrancy and dissipation. The penitentiary was demolished in 1939. A two-billion-dollar project is currently underway to construct a multidisciplinary, business-incubating "Innovation Institute" on the onetime jail site.

The lunatic asylum was described by undercover journalist Nellie Bly in 1887 as a "human rat trap." Beatings and chokings were not uncommon. Residents were stripped naked daily and doused with ice water, for hygienic purposes. Women outnumbered men two-to-one in the institution, as a fair number of them had been committed unwillingly by their husbands; those who arrived sane were frequently driven crazy by the forced doses of morphine and chloral. Soon after Bly's exposé, the asylum was moved to an even more remote location. But a section of the original building, known as The Octagon, remains: it has been converted to upscale condominiums.

It was here at The Octagon that Mona Veigh had come to live in January of 2016. She had arrived seeking quiet and privacy, and present-day Roosevelt Island provided precisely that. No one caused a ruckus on Roosevelt Island, no one wore flashy clothes, and no one made any obtrusive inquiries. It was a place where good-natured families of all ethnicities and creeds jogged happily along the riverwalk, or rode the free Red Bus that wheezed its way every half hour around the island's circumference. It was a lovely, calm, unmenacing neighborhood where nothing out of the ordinary happened. Mona had come to cherish her life here, in all its magnificent drabness. There were people from her past—in fact, just about *all* people from her past—whom she meant to avoid, and up until recently, she had been able to convince herself they had never existed. Yet over the past few weeks, due to a series of inexplicable incidents, Mona Veigh had developed the terrible sense that she was being followed.

On this particular autumn afternoon, a man and a woman in their late twenties—that is, approximately Mona's own age—had been walking about fifty paces behind her along the water's edge. Of course there was nothing odd about this fact in and of itself. After all, there was no reason why a young couple *shouldn't* be enjoying a stroll on the island, feeling the cool breeze on their cheeks, taking in the fine view of Manhattan's east side. And yet everything about these two people felt all wrong.

Over the course of her eight jobless months on Roosevelt Island, Mona had become an expert on its weekday afternoon pedestrians. There were the broad-shouldered nannies, shuttling weary toddlers around in high-tech, impregnable strollers. There were the high school kids just out of class, flirtatiously insulting and kissing and slapping at one another. And there were the retirees—the stoic, multi-sweatered, beautiful retirees. But there were no millennials in neon running shoes and expensive haircuts and matching wool peacoats. Such people were simply not part of the landscape.

Yet at the same time, Mona had some cause to doubt the soundness of her own judgment.

Much as she had enjoyed her months of isolation, she couldn't help but feel that she might be losing her bearings. She had, for instance, not been making the requisite amount of contact with other human beings suggested by mental health experts for maintaining one's sanity. She had not been leaving the island. She had not been bathing as often as is typically considered polite.

Mona Veigh had never been an outgoing or excessively healthy person. She had made her living as a researcher in computational linguistics and got her kicks moonlighting as a scholar of the history of prosody. Neither of these accomplishments, Mona felt, endeared her much to humanity at large. And neither forced her to consort with it much, either. Yet she had made things work for her, in her own way. The company she had founded, Hildegard, had attracted sufficient investment to keep her housed and fed. She was able to devote most of her time to work that interested her. She had even become friendly with a few fellow linguists and literature professors who found her peculiarity more charming than rude.

Then three events took place in short succession that disturbed Mona's equilibrium, each in its own way. The first was that her company was discovered and eventually acquired by an entrepreneur named Avram Parr, thus making her rich. The second was that under Parr's leadership she was then given a "team" to work with, thrusting her into a management position for which she was profoundly ill-suited. The third was that Avram Parr killed himself, sending his company into chaos and leading Hildegard to dissolve.

Becoming rich disturbed Mona because she had no use for the money. Becoming a company woman disturbed her because she had no use for other people. And the dissolution of her company disturbed her because, all of a sudden, she had no use for herself. It had taken her months to regain her comportment and get back to the blissful life of solitude she had known before business ventures diverted her: solitary walks, copious amounts of poetry, and the voluptuous sense that she was protected by great art and by her own steely mind from the ugly excretions of the material world.

This was until two Saturdays past, when Mona could have sworn she'd heard several gentle taps on her door around midnight. She convinced herself that it was her imagination—no one in her building would be calling on her that late, after all—then heard the same rhythmic knocking the following night at the same hour. When she walked to the peephole, however, all she got was a fish-eye's view of the empty hallway. Later that week, Mona saw an unfamiliar man in a suit loitering on a bench outside The Octagon, holding to his face an iPad that she somehow didn't quite believe he was actually reading. He appeared again the next day. And the day after that. Mona then began to see him on a bench at the edge of Four Freedoms Park, at the southern tip of the island, where she took her sunset strolls. But she never got a good look at his face, which he always kept hidden behind the iPad. One afternoon she gathered the nerve to approach him, and he leapt up and power walked, like a stockbroker with a deal to close, toward a nearby parking lot, where he lunged into a black Audi and drove off. That was the last Mona had seen of the man with the iPad. But now there were today's two sinister fashionistas who seemed to be shadowing her every step.

Of course Mona realized it was extravagant to assume that she was being stalked simply because two people behind her were wearing stylish clothes. She wondered if their attire needled her simply because it had hit on one of her sensitive spots. Everything about Mona's own dress was calculated to render her inconspicuous, yet her very lack of affectation, she realized at some level, constituted an affectation of its own—to the point that she occasionally wondered whether her calculated ordinariness might draw the very attention she meant, at least consciously, to repel. Not helping matters was that she had a subtly distinctive appearance that had nothing to do with her clothes. Her skin was uncommonly pale, and her hair was jet black. With round, green eyes and a small nose, her face might have been plain, had it not been for her expressive, mutable mouth, the full lips of which might curl, depending on Mona's mood, to give her a look alternately contemptuous or wry.

She reminded herself that in all likelihood no one was out to get her. She reminded herself that she was not crazy: she was merely an eccentric who ought to leave the house more.

And despite all that, as Mona Veigh made a left on Main Road toward the western side of the island, she saw the two figures behind her take an identical left turn. And she became more certain than ever that she was being followed.

Mona stopped at the river's edge to take in the Manhattan cityscape and collect herself.

She determined that she would not turn again toward her pursuers. If they had indeed been shadowing her and were now walking up the island's western edge, she would let them either confront her or pass by. The sun peeked out for a moment from behind cloud cover and sent a shiver of light across the tall, bland Freedom Tower. Mona had lived, literally, in its shadow until she moved to Roosevelt eight months ago; and even now she resented its bright tumescence and grandiose name. In the apartment in the Financial District where Mona had then resided, it wasn't till late afternoon that the sun would find its way around that glorious testament to the indomitability of the human spirit and financial speculation, and make its way into her bedroom.

It was in that apartment on Liberty Street that Mona developed what she later came to call her *internet problem*: it was as though her computer and phone had begun to exert a mystical pull on her. Part of it, no doubt, was the simple fact that she had suddenly become idle in her joblessness, after years of strenuous intellectual activity, and before she could re-train herself to develop a routine, social networks and live streams and video clips of amazing rainforest frogs swooped in to develop one for her.

But in those weeks there was also a specific train of thought that Mona meant to prevent her mind from following, and her addiction to the net served this function—while satisfying her unconscious by keeping the subject tantalizingly close. This sequence of associations led back to Avram Parr. Specifically, to a conversation Mona had had with him just before he died. Mona could not quite allow herself to follow this thread to any of its logical conclusions. But like a worrisome minor ailment that one obsesses over while at the same time refusing to seek a diagnosis, she couldn't help but become an expert on all the details surrounding Parr's death—details that circled around the specific thought she meant to avoid but never quite touched.

Parr had not even been laid underground before rumors about his manner of death began to spread like malware through various forums and circles of online influence, and Mona found herself powerless to unplug. There was, for instance, the rumor that, before he offed himself, Parr was being hunted by the FBI for some unknown misdeeds, or that the biotech companies Parr funded had run afoul of the cartels, or, most disturbingly, that Parr had not really committed suicide at all—the two injected doses of 12 mg fentanyl reported in the autopsy could not have been used in a self-administered suicide, some argued, because a first dose ought to have incapacitated him to the point where he couldn't have reloaded—and thus some shadow faction had murdered him. Mona had practically memorized these theories and all the other fanciful notions that sprouted up. She woke up with the internet by her side and kept it there, numbing her mind and tiring the joints of her fingers, till the time came to shut her laptop, as one might snuff a candle, and sleep. She set up Google alerts to buzz in her pocket whenever Parr's name was mentioned. She ate Taquitos for dinner and ordered plastic cutlery from Costco in bulk.

STOP ALL THE CLOCKS

By the third straight week of lying in her frameless Tempur-Pedic bed, scouring subreddits for new gossip about shady dealings from Parr's past, Mona realized that her behavior was paralyzing her brain. Whenever she opened a book, her mind unconsciously urged her to scroll down, or to open a new tab. She could no longer think clearly, or concentrate on the words she was reading. And since there was nothing she valued in herself more than the ability to think clearly and to concentrate on words, she realized she was going to have to make a change.

Thus, Roosevelt Island. When Mona moved there, she cut the internet out of her life entirely. She snapped her laptop in half and deposited it, along with her iPhone, into the East River. It did occur to her that this was an overdramatic and environmentally unfriendly solution to her woes. But to watch them splash and sink into the sludgy water was enough of a pleasure that she felt herself justified.

Now, for the last six months, Mona had existed in a state of self-imposed isolation from the world of pop-ups and e-blasts and system updates. She could feel her brain healing, her thoughts slowing down to breathe. But at the same time, she lived in fear of being reconnected with those nefarious ones and zeros. Ads on the bus for cloud computing solutions terrified her. The soft ping of pedestrians' iPhone notifications made her jump. Even the thought of her old coworkers brought a gnawing sickness into her stomach; therefore, she cut off communication with them all. She created a new secure email address at the public library, which she ended up divulging to no one—and so no one wrote.

And no one from her past life had ever come looking for her. Except now there were the two peacoated goons trailing her around the island's riverwalk, whom she felt certain were following her for a reason: they wanted something from her, or they wanted to intimidate her, or perhaps they simply wanted to push her over the railings into the East River.

She turned toward her imagined murderers. They were nowhere in sight. Mona took a deep breath of the marshy air, and felt the muscles of her back twitch as she untensed her body and began to relax. "It's going to be all right," she murmured to herself, but even with this attempt at self-soothing, a tinge of doubt shaded her inflection. She walked quickly back toward the north of the island, where her cozy, lonely condo awaited. She passed by the pizza shop, the Starbucks, the charmingly mediocre Riverwalk Bar & Grill, where drunk construction workers and septuagenarian tuna melt enthusiasts whiled away their afternoons together. She passed by the public garden, the basketball court, the fruit stand: all the mundane little things that made the island feel wholesome and safe.

But more beloved to her than any of these was the little construction site across the entrance to the subway. Unlike the huge renovations on the south end of the island, financed by a multibillion-dollar university and a multibillion-dollar tech firm, the work done here was overseen by the island's cooperative board, so the work done was just about nonexistent.

Beyond the construction tape and past a row of thick bushes, there was a small, secluded area by the water where Mona would go to read, write, or to simply sit quietly when she was feeling overwrought. And as she approached the spot now, she decided this would be just the place to relax.

She sat down gingerly on a steel beam that had been lying in the grass for who knows how long and looked once more across the river toward the borough she'd left behind. From here she could watch the tram, a red steel cable car connecting Roosevelt Island to Manhattan, which glided every ten minutes or so from the island into a landing dock behind a cluster of skyscrapers on the city's east side. There was something comforting about the tram, too. It was unassuming and functional. It followed a strict course of action. And it offered its riders an aesthetic experience that, like the great poems she loved so dearly, was simultaneously brilliant and surefire in its ability to induce vertigo. Riding from the island into the city, one could marvel at Manhattan in all its architectural splendor, before wondering with a lurch of the stomach whether one wasn't being dropped into it a tad too precipitously.

Presently the tramcar dipped out of view. A cozy grayness came over the cityscape as thick cumuli moved over the sun. It became so much more apparent under cloud cover that for all its bright lights, the whole glittering expanse of the city was made up mostly of stone. From the depths of the earth it had been exhumed, and into the earth again it would all someday sink. An errant ball of tinfoil blew across Mona's feet as the breeze picked up again, and she noticed with a chill a rustling sound in the bushes behind her.

It's only the wind, she thought, and felt instantly annoyed that she'd had to resort to a cliché for comfort. But a few moments later the sound of footsteps followed, and Mona would have been glad to take back her comfort, cliché and all. Instead, she turned to see two thin pairs of legs, which led horrifically down toward neon running sneakers, now stepping slowly toward her through the bushes.

(2)

"Oh, our bad!" the woman said, "you must think we're total stalkers."

She introduced herself as Jen and held out her hand. The man beside her only stood there and scratched his face. Mona, feeling that if Jen and her companion were truly deranged then she was best off following their cues for now, rose to greet these gaudily dressed young people who had followed her into a thicket.

Up close, she saw that Jen and the man were tan and well-groomed but not quite svelte. They looked like people who had recently committed to making their appearances Instagram-worthy, but hadn't yet smoothed out the rough edges. Mona shook Jen's hand. Her long nails were decorated with spiral patterns like miniature acrylic labyrinths.

"And this is my colleague Jon," Jen said.

Jon smiled and nodded. He had a patchy, adolescent beard and blank eyes that gave the impression he would prefer to be ogling his phone. But his smile was sheepish and genuine. From the details she had picked up, Mona determined that this was not in fact a murder or a robbery. It was, however, an interaction she meant to terminate as quickly as possible.

"How may I help you?" Mona said, for lack of a more appropriate phrase with which to query her stalkers.

Jen and Jon paused and looked at one another. Their peacoats flapped noisily in the wind.

"Are you Mona Veigh?" Jen asked.

"Yes."

"Well in that case, *super* auspicious to meet you. I've heard through the grapevine from some folks in my network that your start-up was one of the most unique branches of the whole Proserpina constellation."

"Excuse me?"

"Jon and I are content creators, Mona. We're gaining steam to launch a series of longforms on tech mavericks for *Thought Nuggets*, the new culture vertical from Proserpina."

They come in neon running shoes, Mona thought, these murderers of the English language.

"And?" she said.

"And," Jon piped in, "we want to interview you about your experience in tech. We want stories about all the different projects that have flourished under Proserpina, from the time Avram Parr founded it as a humble search engine, until now."

Mona flinched. In this state of tension, *Avram Parr* was the last thing she wanted to hear.

It puzzled her to feel what a strong reaction she still had to the name. She never thought she would've had to grieve over Parr—she wasn't much of a griever, in general. Yet something about his death stayed stuck in Mona's throat. Perhaps, she thought, it was that she felt she had understood him in a way few others did. And, in a way, she had been understood by him.

Whatever other emotions might have been involved, positive or negative, mutual understanding was something too rare and memorable for her to simply shrug off its sudden absence.

At Parr's funeral in New Jersey, for instance, Mona had felt overcome with anger when his relatives got up on stage to eulogize him—they all seemed somehow to have missed his essence. Parr's younger sister, who shared her brother's gauntness and unsociability, but not his cold self-possession, spoke in a halting murmur of Avram's love of innovation. His father, a slightly bowlegged arms trader who had taken young Parr all around the world as he hopped from civil war to civil war, boasted of his son's "stick-to-it-iveness." A maiden aunt told the story of the time Parr programmed her garage door opener to play *Parsifal* on the stereo at full blast whenever a car arrived or embarked.

They had squashed his personality to fit the mold of something they could safely eulogize. *A bit of a geek, perhaps, and a bit remote, but a fine fellow all the same, who used technology to move the world forward and bring us all together.* Yet Mona knew this was as far from the truth as could be. Parr did indeed want to *move the world forward*—but not in a way that these kindhearted mourners in their dark blazers would find palatable. Parr's way of moving the world forward had nothing to do with the vision of humans all across the globe holding hands and singing "Kumbaya." He despised the modern notion that the greatest possible good for the world is simply the easing of human suffering: he thought the world's ambitions should be greater than that. He was an actual idealist: someone who meant to bend the world to fit his ideal, no matter the consequences. What exactly his great ideal was, however, Mona could never formulate precisely. She knew enough to see that he held in contempt the way humans of means currently lived and believed that some better use of human life was possible.

But as for all the rest of it, he had kept it close to his chest.

Mona could assume, however, that *one* part of the scheme was Parr's open war against death—a war which took on a strange poignancy after his suicide. This war of his was one for which Mona had no sympathy. She personally loved to imagine dying: it gave her an enormous comfort to know that life wouldn't simply keep *going on*. But Parr looked at the concept of mortality with the same disdain he held for bureaucratic red tape. It was inevitable, Mona supposed, that a man who believed he could "hack" or "disrupt" all life's troubles would eventually come to believe he could disrupt the very fact that it must end. Apart from AI, the projects Proserpina poured the most money into were genetics firms seeking to write the script for eternal life. Only a few times did Mona ask him explicitly about this obsession of his. Parr had only told her, in his cryptic way, that he thought people in general were biased toward belief that life had a fixed end point, and that he disliked bias in all its forms.

These were precisely the kind of statements from which Mona felt blessedly free now that she had extricated herself from the tech world. On Roosevelt Island, in her cozy condo, among her dozens of shelves of books, tradition reigned, and death was still law. Everything was at its natural human scale. Mona's post-Hildegard season of silence and scholarship had almost been enough to make her forget her life in Parr's world, which she saw now in her mind's eye as the dark swirl of a vortex, sucking up every earthly item in its path.

She turned her thoughts back to the present moment and was relieved to find that it was not Avram Parr who loomed before her—only two overzealous content creators.

"And so you followed me into a thicket?" she asked Jen and Jon.

"No phone, no email, no social. You're very difficult to track down," Jen said, "you must know that."

"That's by design. How did you even know where I live? Or what I look like?"

"Photos were not hard to find," Jon said, "real estate records were a bit trickier. But because you *purchased* the condo, as opposed to leasing, it wasn't *too* too difficult."

"Right. Well I hope you've enjoyed your tour of Roosevelt Island so far. You'll find a mediocre sushi restaurant up the road on your left, and on your right, you've got the decidedly adequate public library branch. But if you don't mind, I'm really not prepared to—"

"Listen, Mona," Jen said, "I realize we're going way out on a prayer here in order to touch base. But honestly, I've never heard of a woman in tech who has the career trajectory that you've had. So could you share a little of your story with us? We won't take up too much of your time."

The gray afternoon had begun to bleed into evening: the west wind brought a chill with it now, and the sun's waning light cast a sheen of gold over the river's dark surface. Had she been alone right now on one of her walks, Mona would have treasured the moment, storing it up for future recollection—perhaps as a symbol of the delights even the end of a good thing can bring about, or of the partnership between darkness and light. But now she only felt worried that she was conversing in a thicket with two near-strangers at dusk as the wind picked up.

"Fine," Mona said, hugging her arms to her chest to stifle a shiver, "but let's go somewhere out of the cold."

*

At the Riverwalk Bar & Grill a dozen flat-screen televisions, installed at various angles across each of the restaurant's walls, vied with each other for the customers' attention. Mona and her interviewers were seated at a high table beside the bar. Jen occupied a place underneath a soccer match and Jon below a telenovela. Mona ordered a basket of mozzarella sticks and a pint of Beck's. She felt that to get through this conversation it would be advisable to be at least partially sedated. Jon set his phone to record and held it in front of Mona's face.

"So we all know," he said, "that the world of tech is striving to connect us in ways we never thought possible. But poetry can connect us too, right? So I was wondering about, like, what's the connection for you between these two ways of connecting?"

Mona felt a muscle in the left side of her face begin to twitch.

"Maybe we'll hit the gas with a query that's a little less open-ended," Jen said, "how did you become the founder of Hildegard in the first place?"

Breathe deeply, Mona said to herself, this will all be over soon. She fixed her gaze above Jen's head, where a shot had bounced off the post.

"I was doing graduate research at Penn on a language-based AI project called Fluid Construction Grammar and spending my off hours at the least lucrative side gig of all time, as a scholar of Elizabethan poetry. After my degree, I got a few grants to do independent linguistics research.

But what I was finding ceased to interest the academic crowd, and so they stopped paying me. When that happened, I said to hell with it, combined my two interests, and tried to see what I could do with AI and poetry. I founded Hildegard, took my show on the road a bit, and managed to interest a few investors. Then Parr made an offer to acquire us that was hard to turn down. I didn't turn it down. I guess he was happy to throw money at just about anything related to artificial intelligence in those days, even if poetry was involved."

"Was founding your own company the plan all along?"

"No. The plan was to study the evolution of blank verse from Surrey to Shakespeare, and then maybe get myself to a nunnery. But somehow I got offtrack."

"That is from *Hamlet*, Shakespeare's landmark tragedy," Jen said to Jon before turning back to Mona, "anyway what do you think Parr saw in the company?"

"I *know* what it's from," Jon said.

Mona recalled the cold evening Parr invited her up to his office for an interview. Other companies that had taken an interest in Hildegard had fobbed her off on lower-level operations officers for their initial meetings, but Parr had wanted to speak with her himself.

"So what *is* a poem?" he asked, the moment she walked through the door, "it is like a normal series of words, only it possesses a pleasing rhythm and timbre?"

"I'm sorry. You're making a joke?"

"My conversation sometimes elicits that response in people—but no, I am not. I suppose they don't have to make a pleasing timbre, do they? They can be the kind that do not rhyme and are difficult to make sense of."

"Poems, you mean. You've never read a poem."

"Not that I can recall. I am familiar with the concept of poems, but I believe I have avoided exposure to them except in cases where, for instance, they were said out loud in my presence."

"It's still sounding a whole lot like you're joking with me," Mona said.

"I do not joke. And I do not read poems."

Mona scanned his face for a smile but didn't find one. Instead she found a boyish earnestness in his pursed lips, and no hint of affect in his cold green eyes.

"Not even in school?" she asked.

"I was homeschooled. My childhood was rather unconventional. I would like to know what you think would be a reasonable sum of money to purchase Hildegard."

"You're telling me you're serious about trying to buy my company when you've never read a poem in your life."

"I do not need to know about poetry to understand your idea, or to know that it is ingenious. Does twenty-five million dollars sound good to you?"

It sounded good to her. Mona took his money, but a slightly smaller amount, on the condition that she would be able to keep her codebase private and only share her results when requested. She never did like people looking over her shoulder when she worked, and she couldn't bear the thought of her heavenly creation being put to ugly, terrestrial uses without her knowledge. Parr assented only when he realized Mona would truly walk away from the deal if he refused—although he did add in a stipulation in her contract that gave him a possible back door into the codebase if he should ever truly need it.

"I never found out exactly what Parr wanted with Hildegard," Mona said to Jen, "in the end he just let me do my research without getting in the way. I suppose he thought the work might have interesting implications. A lot of people in AI are working on very limited, practical questions. How do you build the most thorough approximation of the human eye—that sort of thing. But Parr liked big-picture work. He thought if you studied anything that was compelling to you for long enough, you'd find out what it was good for."

"You must have been excited," Jen said, "when Proserpina brought you into its fold. That's a rare opportunity to have such great support from a founder like Avram Parr."

Mona took a long swig of her beer. The fact was that she had been ambivalent. Not about the money—she was happy to have that—but about the lifestyle that came along with being part of a well-heeled new start-up. The day Parr signed her first check, Mona happily went out to buy herself a new critical edition of Surrey, a new computer, a king-size bed, and a spa day. But a month later, after meeting Parr and the team he'd hired to assist her, Mona began to feel uneasy. She had spent her whole life attempting to maintain autonomy and dignity in a world that now seemed intent on the erosion of both. There had been a reason she studied obscure things: that way no one knew enough about them to bother her. Now she was out in the open, sharing pho lunches with developers who sat in ergonomic chairs and didn't read anything but their newsfeeds and the latest research relevant to their field. Worst of all was Parr's thin-lipped smile when he'd show up for their monthly one-on-one and invariably ask: "Read any good poems lately?" This was his idea of a joke. He told her that since their interview he had been prioritizing his ability to make jokes.

"It was a wonderful opportunity," she murmured.

Jen and Jon nodded in agreement. They had both ordered a cup of coffee—after being informed that the diner served neither cappuccino nor almond latté—and they had both left their cups untouched.

"And could you describe to us briefly the work itself?" Jon asked excitedly, "you created a large language model that wrote poetry. Is that more or less correct?"

"More or less," Mona said, "but with the emphasis on less. Anybody can create a bot that writes poetry if you define poetry, as many people do, as obscure prose with arbitrary line breaks. Google 'bot poetry' and you'll find all varieties of that sort of thing."

"But there was something about Hildegard that took the creative act further?"

"I should think so. The program is named after Hildegard von Bingen, a mystical, possibly schizophrenic nun who invented her own language, recombining different phonemes to build a lonely bridge toward God. And I intended for my program to match the eccentricity of its namesake. It is not a simple algorithm where you input one variable in order to spit out another, but a supervised learning system, intelligent and creative, which learned according to parameters even *I* don't fully understand."

"How would you not understand them?" Jen said.

"If you'll listen," Jon said, "she's about to tell us. Yes, how would you not understand them?"

Mona grimaced and cleared her throat.

"Think of a small child. This child will learn language at a miraculous rate, but the way he or she does this is still largely mysterious to us. What's clear, however, is that children have some inborn system for acquiring language. You don't tell a child: here's what a noun is, here's what a verb is, etc. The kid just *gets* it."

Jen nodded solemnly, while Jon only scratched his beard.

"And so, my idea," Mona continued, "was that the capacity for poetry was inborn the same way the capacity for language is. Which is to say that, given a tutor—in this case, me—a poetic grammar could emerge spontaneously from a machine. So I gave Hildegard a set of parameters by feeding it lines of poetry and prose I'd culled from the corpus of all English literature, including metadata to mark which lines were iambic, which had feminine rhymes, et cetera. Building off that, Hildegard combined its own lines of verse, just as a child or a novice poet might. I would respond by sorting through a sample of lines Hildegard proposed and letting it know whether the lines were appropriate to a given poem, both metrically and semantically. Hildegard's poetry, lo and behold, emerged much the same way ours has. For instance, it began by being much more inclined toward alliterative verse than to rhyme, because that was an easier pattern to discover. Typically, large language models are clumsy when asked to write poetry. Hildegard was not, because it learned on its own, just as a great chess engine like AlphaZero became the greatest in the world, simply by extrapolating from the rules of the game."

"I read a summary from our files," Jon said, "explaining that you trained Hildegard to be able to write all different kinds of poems on demand, from sonnets to pop songs."

"That's partially right," Mona said, "I let it write the poems it wanted to, and then I allowed it to determine on its own what was poetic and what wasn't, according to a few basic parameters. The determinations it made were idiosyncratic and inconsistent—just as they were in the works of Chaucer or Skelton or even Shakespeare: poets who were inventing English poetry merely by expressing their thoughts as best they could. Regularity of form was something that had to emerge from Hildegard just as it had to emerge in poetry created by humans. But once consistency emerged, then a whole canon of sonnets, of blank verse monologues, of brisk rhyming couplets were all produced. This is why it seems like it can produce these things on command; really, though, it's just tapping into its own inborn penchant for creativity."

"Wow," Jon said, "it sounds like work that's got some really broad applications. I can see why Parr would have been such a huge supporter of yours. Have you been working on the same project since the time he was killed?"

Mona was about to answer that she had not been working on the same project—she had not been working on any tech projects at all—before she stopped herself and glared into Jon's dull eyes. She repeated his last phrase in her head to make sure she had heard it correctly.

"Did you say 'since he was *killed*?'"

(3)

"Since he killed himself," Jen interrupted, "Jon meant since he killed himself."

"Yes," Jon added, "I meant, since he was killed—by, uh, himself."

"Yes," Jen said, "since he was killed by *himself*. Jon has a tendency to state things with a lexical creativity of his own."

They all sat for a moment in silence. The telenovela had gone to break. The soccer match wound up in penalties. A series of images unfurled in Mona's mind: she imagined a beautiful spring afternoon, the day of Parr's funeral. In her fantasy, he was being lowered slowly into the ground. But just as the last clods of dirt fell over his face, Parr lifted his head and winked at Mona. A man in a suit—was he the man with the iPad?—shuffled past the gravesite.

Mona returned from her dreamscape and looked fearfully at Jen and Jon. For the moment they seemed to have gone back from being harmless fools to stalkers full of malign intent. Their presence now brought to Mona's mind all the strangeness of Parr's death and its ramifications in her own life. She tried to speak but could not.

The memory she had tried hardest to repress now floated back to the surface. This one was not a fantasy, but balefully true. It had taken place last autumn, when Parr had come by Hildegard's Midtown offices for a one-on-one.

It was nearly 9:00 p.m., and only Mona and Parr remained in the building.

"What would you say to me," Parr blurted out just as he sat down across from Mona, "if I told you I had to go away for a while."

"You need someone to bump off a bookie for you?"

"I do not gamble. Not in that way, at least."

"You should take it up. I bet you could learn how to count cards in just a day or two."

"Perhaps. But money itself has never interested me."

"That must be a relief to the Bellagio. Now are we going to do my review? Before we start, I want you to know two things about the incident with the vending machine. First of all, those fancy almond bars are incredibly addictive. Second of all, when Spencer hacked together an override code, he assumed that we owned the thing. No one realized there were any third parties involved—"

"You knew that already, did you not?" Parr said, "that money itself does not interest me. You understand me well enough to understand that."

"So I'm guessing we're *not* going to do my review now."

"Your work has been satisfactory on all counts. The reason money itself does not interest me is that what I want from life cannot be bought. I have the sense that it is the same way for you."

"I hate to break it to you, Avram," Mona said, "but I've never really been one for heart-to-hearts."

"In that case I will keep this matter as brief as it needs to be. But I need to ask you an important question."

Mona stiffened in her chair. She did not know what was going on, but whatever it was, she didn't care for it.

"A large percentage of people who know who I am think that I am evil," Parr said. "I am certain of this. I have collected the data. These people see that I have a lot of money. But they do not see me donating to popular charities—charities that will squander the money on the salaries of useless administrators. They see that am I interested in social problems, but they do not see me endorsing the smiling political candidates who have spent their lives learning how to manipulate them. They see instead that I have a vision, but they don't know what it is. Perhaps that it is how the notion of evil came into the world. The first human tribe said, 'we need a word for that one over there, who is thinking something, but we do not know what it is.'"

"I'm not," Mona said, "hearing a question word."

"When people perceive evil there is no accounting for how they might behave. I now have some difficult choices to make. I may be forced out of my own company."

"That's hard to imagine."

"Whether you can imagine it is immaterial. What I want to ask is this: If I left, would you think of coming with me? As business partners, let us say. We could start something entirely new."

This was not what Mona had expected. She gave Parr a long look up and down. He cut the figure of an adolescent who had once held promise physically, but instead of filling out, shot upward through the torso while his spindly legs stayed behind in teenage limbo. His close-cropped black hair had the sheen of a boy's. His hands were pale and delicate. The only feature of Parr's that gave a clue to his character were his gray-green eyes, deep-set and ellipsoid, which always appeared to be looking just a few feet past whatever object they were trained on. Mona took note of these eyes from the moment she met Parr. As it happened, in their shade and shape they were remarkably similar to her own.

"I don't really—" Mona began

"I realize that you do not see yourself primarily as a businessperson. I realize that, for whatever strange reason, you prefer poetry to world-changing technological innovations. But I have observed you and I believe you see the world the same way that I do."

Mona felt the blood rush to her face. She had the sudden urge to get as far away from the office as possible.

"I don't know what you mean," she lied, "and the answer to your question is *no*."

Parr nodded and stood up. His expression betrayed nothing.

"It may be a long time before I see you again. I cannot say precisely when. Thank you for all your hard work on Hildegard."

He flew back that week to Proserpina's headquarters in Cupertino, and the following week he was dead. Mona never consciously believed that their conversation had any direct relation to his death, but the notion had now begun to fester in her mind. Mona knew rationally that it didn't make sense for Parr to kill himself, and she knew with a part of herself deeper than rationality that there was something about her final conversation with him that didn't add up. Maybe there was a hidden meaning to his question that she didn't understand. Or maybe he had simply meant to tell her that night that he was in danger.

*

Mona finished off her beer with a long gulp and frowned at her afternoon interlocutors.

"Let me ask you a question," she said suddenly, "since you're the first Proserpina people I've seen in months. When Parr died, he must have personally owned close to a billion dollars' worth of Proserpina stock. But no one seems to know who his beneficiaries were. His will was a black box. So where did all that money go?"

"Huh?" Jon said.

"Where did it go to? It couldn't have simply disappeared."

"Mona," Jen said, "we're just content creators. Well, *I'm* content creative director. But we're not lawyers. We wouldn't have the foggiest trace of an idea."

"Who would know?"

"His lawyers, surely. Or higher-ups at Proserpina."

"Such as?"

"I'll tell you what," Jen said, "why don't you come by the co-working station where my team's having an all hands tomorrow afternoon? In the meantime, I'll do some recon to see who you could liaise with."

"That would be just fine," Mona said.

"Can we get back to the interview?" Jon said. "I have a few more questions."

"I'm afraid I've reached the end of my interview tolerance," Mona said.

"But we've just gotten started," Jon said. His face formed into a puppy-dog pout.

"Let's at least have one more question," Jen said. "We've certainly all gone through enough trouble just to be in the same room together."

Mona sighed. "One more," she said.

"Do you think," Jon blurted out, pushing his phone unnecessarily close to Mona's face, "that Hildegard's poetry will ever be better than human poetry? Or will human genius always be better?"

"Actually I'm not sure I would attribute *any* great poems to human genius," Mona said. "William Blake claimed that his verse arrived by way of the angels, who would chatter at him for days at a time. Milton told of a 'Celebrated Patroness' who 'dictates to me my unpremeditated verse.' Housman said his poems popped into his head automatically after he downed a couple pints and went for a walk in the woods. Go back to the first great poem in the canon, how does it begin? 'Sing *through* me, muse.' Now, if humans can act as conductors for whatever divine-seeming force writes poetry *through* them, maybe a machine can too. For now Hildegard's poems come off a bit as parody. But that's no knock against them. We've got so far away—with our listicles and thoughtsicles and brain droplets and what not—from the heart of what language can do, that we may need a little extra estrangement to bring us back around to the crux of things. Language is mysterious that way: there's a magic to it, but no pat formula for practicing that magic."

"But can language really be that mysterious?" Jon asked. "I mean, if we're teaching computers how to use it?"

Mona knew she was being goaded into an extra question, but she could not help herself.

Much as she wanted to get away from the two of them, she suddenly felt the need to justify her way of life—not only to them, but to the world at large, with which she felt she was becoming increasingly out of touch. She wanted to show them the grandeur and inviolability of poetic inspiration. She wanted to prove that the questions she'd been asking herself all this time were worthwhile.

"Let me give you an example," Mona said. "Take even the most banal sentence. Let's say 'The sky is blue.' On the one hand nothing could be simpler. On the other hand it's both infinitely complex and shrouded in mystery, as strange and potent as any magical spell. 'Sky,' for instance, could mean a hundred different things: from the chemical compounds of the atmosphere to the residence of the gods to the big pale sheet above the mountains that thunders and cries. Or it could mean *that* slice of sky there in the distance. Or *that* one right next to it.

"Now take 'blue.' Blue is a spectrum, a state of mind, a party trick performed by a septillion neutrinos in your brain. And then don't get me started on what the meaning of the word 'is' is. It turns out, once you think about it, that *all* words are metaphors. I can never actually communicate the concrete thingness of *any* word—whether it's 'sky' or 'blue' or 'red rose' or 'necromancy.' But when I use those words they are *like* the things themselves, just enough for you to follow. If you ask me, all language is a just a lonesome prayer that we and the world actually exist, a cry in the wilderness to the god of meaning. And, miraculously, that god hears us. When I say 'The sky is blue,' it's a miracle that you have any sense at all of what I'm saying. It's a miracle that I can induce a feeling in other humans with this series of abstract grunts and yawps and plosives. We almost never stop to think just how strange language is, how poetic and potent and recondite and prayerful just to say 'The sky is blue!' The possibilities are limitless. Someday a great poet may write an epic in which everything hinges on that single line!"

Her questioners remained silent for a moment. The sun had descended and the restaurant had all but emptied out. Jon's face, for some reason, had gone white. Mona stared at the two of them, begging with her eyes for some sign of comprehension.

STOP ALL THE CLOCKS

"Um," said Jon, rubbing his beard, "I didn't want to interrupt you, but it looks like none of that got recorded. Hit the wrong button, I guess. Can you try to repeat all of that? You were saying something about how, um, the sky is blue, and that's poetry?"

(4)

The next day Mona took the train into Manhattan. The co-working space Jen had mentioned occupied the ground floor of a handsome Village brownstone. A plaque on the outer wall congratulated the co-workers therein for "maintaining the neighborhood's radical, artistic cultural legacy." Through the long glass window there could be seen two low wooden tables stretching across the main room. A half dozen young people sat at them and stared into MacBooks. Mona took a deep breath. She buzzed the door, and Jen arrived at the entrance to usher her in.

"I *seriously* wanna apologize about the recording glitch," she said. "We can do a mulligan on the interview any time."

The six co-workers co-sitting at the table looked up with evident annoyance at the notion that anyone in their vicinity should be doing anything but typing rhythmically at a laptop. Mona frowned at as many of them as she could simultaneously.

"I promise you that won't be necessary."

"I hope you're not mad. At *Thought Nuggets* one of our core philosophies is to give team members the green light to take initiative on their own passions. Jon and I had both been ultra-curious about your career as an outlier and just *had* to find you."

"You might end up as something of an outlier yourself if you keep stalking people."

"Stalking is a strong word, Mona. I prefer *investigative content creation*."

"Well if you must create content, please do so elsewhere. And forget my email address, if you don't mind. Speaking of which, had any bright recollections about Christian Rosecrans since we last spoke?"

This revelation of the name *Rosecrans* was the one good thing to come from Jen and Jon's attempt at content creation. Mona had given Jen her email in order to coordinate the rendezvous now taking place—a meeting with Natalie Kulak, Proserpina's Head of People—and she had also prevailed on Jen to send a list of police and medical officials Mona could contact about Parr's death. Mona had hoped, as she made her way to Roosevelt Island's quaint public library branch, that Jen's list would allay her suspicions. She had a particularly delicious Jacobean drama waiting for her at her condo, and the clear autumn afternoon was crisp with melancholy.

But the trip to the library only further inflamed Mona's suspicion. She opened up Jen's email at one of the public computers, and, after copying down the address of the co-working space, turned her attention to the list of names. She ran her eyes up and down it as though, understood properly, it might return Parr from the dead. The names on the Google Doc were:

Toya Clay
Chief Medical Examiner
tclay@ocme.nyc.gov
212-487-1351

Mark Rollins
First Deputy to the Chief Medical Examiner
mrollins@ocme.nyc.gov
212-487-2335

Detective Jerry Aldo
212-229-1968 [ext 42]
Midtown Precinct South
357 W. 35th Street, New York, NY 10001

Mona copied down the email addresses and numbers in her notebook and was about to release herself back into the mellow afternoon when a tingle occurred at the nape of her neck. She had known this tingle before: it told her to trust her own sense of unease. A mischievous idea came into her head, as though voiced from above. Mona moved her cursor over to the "Document History" option and clicked on a version of the same document Jen had sent, but from eight months prior, shortly before Parr's death. Scrolling down to the bottom of the page now revealed one more name, a red horizontal line struck through it to indicate it had been deleted in the final version. That name was:

Christian Rosecrans
Hematology
822-0929

Mona began a search for the identity of this redacted man, bereft even of an area code to accompany his phone number. But no matter how deep she dug, there did not appear to be a Googlable human named Christian Rosecrans, to say nothing of a hematologist by such a name. (There was, rather unhelpfully, an apocryphal legendary character with a similar appellation, however.) The public library computers each timed out after a forty-five-minute session, and so Mona hopped from monitor to monitor to chase her sleuthing high. No other unaccompanied adults were in the library branch on this weekday afternoon—only nannies teaching children to see Spot run and not to chew the bindings, and the thirtysomething employee with bags under his eyes and tufts of hair on his thick neck, scribbling away in a Moleskine at the library's Welcome Station. Eventually he became annoyed by Mona's hopping back and forth between computers, and approached her to ask:

"Is there a research question I might help you with?"

"As a matter of fact there is," Mona surprised herself by answering. "How did Avram really die?"

He gave her a blank stare—there was nothing out of the ordinary about erratic behavior in a public library—and then walked away to commence tidying up the books on the New Fiction shelf, daintily adjusting each book so that its spine aligned with its neighbors. Mona later surmised that he himself was some kind of madman, for when she sneaked a glance at his Moleskine on the way out, she found that on a fresh page of the notebook he had written only the date and time, and the inscription:

01001000 01100101 00100000 01100100 01101001 01100100 01101110 00100111 01110100.

*

"I'm telling you, Mona," Jen said as she ushered Mona toward the sad-looking "fun" area of the co-working station, featuring games for adult children and a beer tap that had run dry, "I must have been on a total Ambien jag or something when I wrote that *Christian Rosecrans* name. No idea what it was meant to infer. Or maybe—I know!—my mom hopped onto my laptop when I wasn't looking and typed that in. She's had loads of specialists since her rhinoplasty last June."

"Why would your mother have been on your laptop? Doesn't she have her own?"

"We're a *super* close family, Mona. Anyway, it's been mega enlightening to shoot the breeze with you, but I have a webex at three, and I need to work in some cardio first. Feel free to chill here until Natalie arrives. She's quite the game changer, too, actually. Before she got promoted to Head of People she was on the front lines of a Proserpina umbrella company called

CRISPR-X. They altered people's DNA and stuff. Sort of dystopian—but in a good way, you know?"

*

A tall woman with a severe look on her face approached. "You must be Mona Veigh," she said.

"You must be the people header."

"Excuse me?"

"Natalie Kulak, Head of People?"

"Right. Still getting used to the title. Listen, it's depressing in here, no? Too much silence. What do you say we walk?"

They strolled down busy Sixth Avenue, past tired-looking street hawkers and empty storefronts—the shells of small businesses waiting to be filled in by Duane Reades or banks. The bell tower of the Jefferson Market Library gonged 2 o'clock. On its wide steps a man with tattered shoes sat holding *How to Win Friends and Influence People* upside down in front of his face.

"I thought it'd be just as well if we got out of there," Natalie said. "Sometimes I get the sense that all the data mining that goes on around there has expanded to include bugging the walls."

Natalie's face brightened now that they'd left the co-working space, and she walked with the brisk ease of a real New Yorker, unafraid to side-swipe slow-moving tourists. She was poised and efficient-looking, with short blonde hair pulled back into a bun and the faintest trace of an Eastern European accent. Mona liked her already.

"The sad thing is," Natalie continued, "six months ago if I'd talked about the place being bugged I'd have been joking. Now I'm not so sure. Everyone at Proserpina is so paranoid since Parr died. Here's a health food place I like. They've got a *fantastic* salad bar."

The two of them filled up their plastic containers with kale salad and quinoa and pale root vegetables that Mona could not quite identify.

"Paranoid about what?" Mona asked.

They sat down at a table in the back corner of the shop and leaned in to hear one another as they spoke in half-whispers. Mona thought they must have seemed like the people one sometimes finds ensconced in lonely New York diners, chattering quietly for hours about the government's plans for global mind control, or secret plans to overthrow the reptilian elite.

"I'll put it this way. Jen and Jon told me you wanted to know about the allocation of Parr's shares after he died. Well, you're not the only one. I take it you were broken up about his death?"

"That's what Jen and Jon told you?"

"Something like that. They said you were living like a hermit."

"That's not strictly because of Avram Parr. But it's true that I spiraled a bit. I'm not the sort of person who has a million friends, you know. He was someone I could talk to. If something untoward really did happen to him, I'd feel like it's my job to prove it."

All of a sudden Mona felt embarrassed before Natalie. When they had been striding down Sixth Avenue she had felt her equal: two professionals on their way to a lunch meeting to discuss business. But now she had reminded them both of her chosen estrangement from this world.

"What *else* did Jen and Jon tell you?"

"Not much," Natalie said. "Jen mentioned that you were writing a poem about the sky being blue, or something like that."

Mona picked at a piece of greens that she realized had got stuck between her teeth. "Must have been a mistake."

"In any case, lay it all out for me. What are your concerns?"

Mona recounted the interview about Hildegard in the thicket and Jon's slip-up, along with the unaccounted-for name she had discovered in the Google Doc. She abstained from mentioning her general sense of unease and paranoia these past few weeks.

"Where were Hildegard's offices?" Natalie asked.

"Midtown East. What's that got to do with it?"

"It reminds me of something that happened to me back at my old job."

"X-Fryer?" Mona said.

Natalie laughed quietly and made a motion to smooth her hair back over her temples, though not a strand was out of place.

"CRISPR-X. CRISPR is an acronym for 'clustered regularly interspaced short palindromic repeats.' Gene sequences that help us splice DNA together, is the short version. We were a biotech company Parr bought back in 2010. A big bet for a crew of Bay Area dropouts, but that's how he liked 'em. The point is, even back then you needed about six dozen different types of verification to get anywhere *near* our lab. And the people who understand the science well enough to make use of what they saw there would only just about fill out this cafeteria."

"Okay..."

"So just a month or so before Parr died, this mysterious guy in a suit starts showing up in meetings. Doesn't say a word, hardly seems to blink, but he's absolutely, one hundred percent... *there*."

"Go on."

"He hangs around for a few weeks, and gradually I start to let it go. Whatever, there's a new guy nobody told me about. But then one day he's replaced by a *different* guy. Eerily similar-looking, like they could have been identical twins. You'd really have to be paying attention to notice it—but I swear to you, they're different. This second guy, for instance, has got an abnormally long ring finger, an inch or so longer than his middle digit. So I go to my boss and say 'who are these two new guys?' 'What new guys?' my boss says, 'there are no new guys.' I'm about to go insane at this point, and a few other people on my team are weirded out too. I pressed as much as I could, and all I got from my boss was that there had been *one* guy, a higher-up at Proserpina who'd come to check up on things. Said his name was Henry Munio. Of course there's nothing I could find about anyone with that name. Anyway, the guy stopped showing up just the day after I made a big stink about it. Two weeks later I was promoted out of there."

The two of them finished their meals and put their sullied plastic receptacles in the recycling. The whole area was redolent with the hybrid odor of cleaning supplies and detoxifying herbs. Natalie touched Mona's elbow lightly as they made their way toward the door.

"The reason I asked about your offices is this. My *hunch* is that something extra is going on at some of Proserpina's real estate. I've done my share of sleuthing at the old CRISPR-X offices, but I can't get into these other places without raising hackles. So I'm hoping you'll drop by Hildegard's old building for me and let me know if you find anything interesting. I'll do the same if I come across anything. How can I get in touch with you?"

"Well," Mona said.

"Well?"

"You don't happen to have a carrier pigeon, do you?"

"You're telling me you don't have a phone."

"It makes avoiding robocalls blissfully easy."

Natalie smiled indulgently as she angled her feet toward the door.

"Get a phone, would you?" she said, "and text me when you've got it. Back to the grind for me now. I can only hide out here with you for so long."

*

How nice it was to have a prospective new friend. As she contemplated it, Mona felt her recent loneliness not as a pleasure but as a deep pain, and sifted back through the story of how it had come to exist. Not long ago she had known the satisfaction—or, rather, had felt it unconsciously—of being part of a milieu. How had it transpired that Mona now found herself separated from them? The same way Hemingway said a man goes broke: gradually and then all at once. Mona had always felt a dark desire to lose the worldly contacts that kept her firmly among the living. A pull, as it were, toward the abyss. How deep is the abyss, really? she'd wondered at the time. Now she had jumped.

Mona had made friends quickly and easily with the other clever or artistic urbanites who clustered together at her leafy New England college. They had seemed to find one another through a shared acidity. And then like ants they assembled, quickly and without thinking, into formation.

They took part in a select number of acceptable professions after college. One could bum around, one could study art and literature, one could work odd jobs, one could even work a well-paying job so long as it was in a sufficiently mercenary manner. One could strip, as some clever girls Mona knew did; or one could even turn tricks. But beyond that one was certainly not meant to go into *business*.

This, Mona would reflect, was the seed from which her ostracism grew and flowered. In college an interest in computer programming could be considered a cute, eccentric hobby by the milieu. But once Mona turned to it professionally (and where else was she to turn? She was not nearly good enough at ass-kissing, she realized soon enough, for academia) she became decidedly declassé.

Interestingly it was not making money itself that her friends objected to. Annalisa, one friend who "danced" and dabbled in even more strenuous varieties of exotic entertainment, did quite well for herself and made a show of living luxuriously. But she was spared the scorn of the milieu because there was something cynical, perhaps even ironic, about her enjoyment of wealth. To say nothing of the fact that she was debasing herself (though no one would have said so) in order to acquire it—which was even more *chic*. And of course there was nothing gauche at all about availing oneself of parents' money for trips to country houses or to France.

Could it have been that earnestness itself was the anathema of the milieu? A business venture was inherently earnest; Mona could not afford to be sardonic with investors about Hildegard, and perhaps that earnestness came to permeate her personal life as well—with disastrous results. Back then she had one close friend, Casey, a talented sculptor. Casey had studied visual art in college. She had devoted herself to work. And yet she could not allow herself to love her work simply and innocently. She was ashamed of it: ashamed, Casey explained, of the *uselessness* of it. They spoke about it once in Casey's studio, a dim and dingy affair in the Bronx that was filled, Mona thought, with the most strange and wondrous clay creatures. Casey continued her self-divided life as a sculptor for three years out of college; then she went to CUNY law school, seeking to help the helpless, and became rather bitter.

Although Mona was ambivalent about the tech world, she was by no means self-divided on the subject of her work. Building Hildegard was an introverted activity that required all her creativity, and thus it brought her joy. And for all her misgivings about the computers that were enveloping life, she felt comfortable, in one particular sense, with the programmers: They cared about the thing in itself. That is, they were not looking over their shoulders, as Casey had done, at the question of how what they were doing might be perceived. They were working on problems because the problems were there. They were almost like artists in their passion for the minute details of their projects and their antipathy toward those peskiest of all variables: people.

*

She went straight to the Verizon store and bought a gleaming new phone. It took all of fifteen minutes. The salesman welcomed her with saccharine receptivity to all queries, and his shiny black hair wobbled like a cake on a tray as he went back and forth from the stockroom to the showroom to display to Mona the latest models. Only a few minutes after she removed it from its stiff, smooth cardboard, the phone connected Mona to the world via a 4G LTE digital network. Radio waves from the sleek device in her hands sent data to cell towers that had now multiplied so fruitfully as to span the entire globe. Mona sat down on a bench in Washington Square to play with her new device.

It felt good to give in to the flow of data that characterized the phone: the quick swipes and flicks of the finger that felt like wizardry, the smug knowledge that she could access any fact in an instant. Mona was sober enough in her thinking to know that the waves emitting from the phone were not in fact palpable, yet she could swear she felt them washing over her, pulling her in their tide back toward modern life. She noted to herself that she must be careful not to drown. Mona now had someone, in Natalie, who was depending on her. She felt glad about it. Glad, too, that they were now connected by these radio waves that could break down facts and feelings into digestible signs and symbols that were communicated in an instant. She looked up from tinkering with her device to observe her surroundings. From her seat at the park's central fountain, she had a fair view of each of its four quadrants, which she knew well: Mona often made use of the big university library only a stone's throw away, and so she had spent many hours lingering in this park with a book. She had its geography memorized. At the northwest corner were the weed dealers, shuffling around in loops, muttering "smoke, smoke" to anyone who would listen. At the southwest corner were the chess hustlers, each sitting regally before his own little eight-by-eight square kingdom. Southeast led to the library and was swarmed with students. And Northeast was home to the skaters, who gravitated toward the ever-grindable stone base of a monument to Garibaldi.

This, at least, was how Mona saw the four quadrants in her mind's eye. But now as she scoped it from her fountain lookout, what she saw disturbed her. No one was doing anything but looking at their phones. The chess players were sitting silently at their chess stations texting, or maybe playing online chess. The students were lying in the grass with their phones hugged to their faces. The skaters had clumped together to watch a video. Even the drug dealers appeared to have left off making their rounds. Of course Mona had observed this situation before on trains and in offices, and she had skimmed the dismayed thinkpieces bemoaning that no one paid attention any longer to the world around them because they were too absorbed in their phones.

But what struck Mona now was not curmudgeonliness or nostalgia, but the feeling that an invisible string had wrapped itself around them all and was moving them about like marionettes. A series of bleeps and bloops, and the chess player picked up his phone. A digitally compressed voice emitted from the screen, and the skater laughed. A ping, and the students rapped away madly with their thumbs. Why had no one noticed this before? That it was, at this point, the devices that were calling the shots, and the people were the technology by which the devices communicated. They were all characters in a story being orchestrated through their three-inch by six-inch radio frequency cue cards. It was evidently an epic and mysterious story, spanning populations all across the globe. It was endlessly fascinating and wholly immersive. It was tragedy and comedy, love story and thriller all rolled into one. But who had written it?

Hildegard 2.0's Modern Lyric

you were alone with your words in your dark world. you—
an island, entire of itself, illumed
by lamplight, buffered against the river's tides
then death diminished you
others got involved

they came to your island, shouted you—
just a moment, you!
in your peripheral vision, among the bushes or lurking in the parking lot
they wait for you—
with a purpose that is no purpose
while you fear the fear
that haunts the innermost haunts
of soul and mind
constituting the ache and the worth
of you—you tried to understand
what they wanted with you taking
into consideration all the history
that circumscribes instantiates constitutes you—

who were you before he or she or it or them told you to be you?
could a detective uncover certain fine traces of you?
as night falls, the emptiness expands
God works out gradually
what He has determined absolutely
he has determined you will die
and you will sink back

into the soup of he and she and them and it
and the all-pervasive all-knowing I

(5)

"Oh, you see all types," Detective Aldo said, "after a while they begin to blend together. Sometimes literally. About ten years ago up in Spuyten Duyvil we found a couple of poor bastards melted together hip to hip with a welding flame, like a pair of Siamese twins. Conjoined, I suppose, is the term I should use. But I don't mean to be grotesque. Real acts of evil all end up looking alike, is what I'm trying to say—just like corpses. It's living, law-abiding folks who seem peculiar to someone in my line of work after a while. Almost makes a man want to get sentimental, imagining those millions of upstanding citizens taking bassoon lessons or baking chicken cacciatore right now as we speak. It's hard to know just how they do it. But some things are meant to remain a mystery, I guess."

The sun, now setting between two midtown skyscrapers, glared through the window of Aldo's fourteenth-floor office and lit up his childishly round face. Mona had called all the numbers on Jen's list, and Detective Jerry Aldo was the only one who had picked up. He was a man of about 250 pounds, none of it muscle, dressed in a dirty gray suit. His uppermost coat button threatened to explode against the weight of his paunch. Mona, who sat in a too-large office chair across him at his desk, wondered if she should take cover.

She'd thought she would butter up the detective by asking about his line of work, and thereby make him more likely to answer her questions.

Mona had imagined a tight-lipped, well-kempt professional—not a ragged, loquacious behemoth.

"Generally we prefer not to go much beyond the official write-up, even after a case is closed. But it's nice to have someone who isn't a criminal or a cop 'round the place every once in a while. Keeps things civilized."

His office was lined nearly wall to wall with towers of banged up bankers boxes, overstuffed manila file folders, legal pads covered with a red pen's wild scrawl, and other office detritus of indeterminate function. Pictures of a little boy in baseball and Cub Scout uniforms stood framed on the desk. There were also pictures of the boy with Aldo and a dowdy woman who must have been the mother. A badly done oil painting of the Madonna and child, with the novice's enthusiasm for gaudy Fauvist colors, hung on the wall to the detective's left.

"I do appreciate it," Mona said. "I know you must be busy. I just had a few questions about the case of Avram Parr. You see—"

"Parr, Parr, Parr. He was the one who asphyxiated himself with the weird sex thing?"

"What? Um, no," Mona said, "no, you've got things mixed up. Avram Parr, according to the official record, committed suicide by means of fentanyl injection, but the issue, to my mind, is—"

"Parr! Now I remember. Oh, that case. The technology guy. Stupid, how could I have forgotten. It was in the papers, no?"

"He was well known in certain circles."

"Well, I hope it doesn't disappoint you, but that Parr was a suicide cut and dry as Jack's Links Jerky. Fentanyl overdose. He planned it all out cleanly and meticulously, like the science nerd that he was. I do get names mixed up now and again, but once I've got the right one, all the details flood back to me."

"I see," Mona said.

Detective Aldo's mouth hardly seemed to move when he spoke. His voice was steady and soft, as though he were offering absolution. The only visible motion in him was the rising and falling of his enormous chest.

Mona decided to change tack and play the concerned citizen: direct, serious, and unwilling to be diverted from the path to justice.

"I have reason to believe you're incorrect," Mona said, "I mean there are indications, I've found, that Avram Parr has been murdered."

Aldo finally stirred. He cocked his head and scrunched up his eyes into little crescent moons.

"You know what's the real doozy," he said, "I went on one of those fad diets three months ago and now I've gained another twenty-five pounds. It's starting to look like I was better off gorging myself on Krispy Kremes and Ding Dongs."

"I'm sorry? What does that have to do with Avram Parr?"

"Not a thing, I'm afraid." Aldo turned to the painting of the Virgin and Christ Child. "Do you ever pray?"

"Do I *pray*? No, as a matter of fact I don't. But I really don't understand—"

"I do. I pray to get thin. I pray and I pray and he doesn't answer. That's how I know He's real. Only a really two-bit God would answer such a stupid prayer."

Mona looked down at her feet, as though embarrassed by the boastful comment of a child.

"I'm kidding with you, Mona," Aldo said. "The fact is, I just oughtta eat healthy and get myself a StairMaster. God doesn't have so much to do with it. Would you like coffee, by the way?"

"I would like to know the facts surrounding the death of Avram Parr. With as much detail as you can provide."

But Aldo was already up out of his chair. The node of his heft, it turned out, wasn't so much at his chest as at his upper groin: it jut out like a fanny pack.

"I'm up to six or seven cups a day. The irony is there's no surer way to make yourself dog tired all the time. How well did you say you knew Avram Parr?"

"We were colleagues."

"That's right, you mentioned the fact on the phone. I just wanted to ask—I hope you don't find me coarse—if there hadn't been something . . . a little more."

Sex, Mona thought, always sex. You can come dressed in a shapeless hoodie and jeans.

You can come as a concerned citizen. You can come to investigate the cause of a former employer's suspicious death. And still these men want to know first and foremost: has there been sex? The deep groan of Aldo's Keurig machine sputtered and gave way to a trickle.

"Nothing more," Mona said, "and to be honest with you, the suggestion of it disgusts me."

"Forgive my coarseness. It's in my nature to ask questions, is all. You know, people in a business like mine just can't turn off the switch. Sorry to have offended you."

"I didn't say I was offended. I said I was disgusted."

A look of genuine dismay passed across Aldo's face. He folded himself slowly into his office chair. In his enormous hand his coffee mug looked like a teacup for a doll.

At that moment he no longer seemed to Mona merely an obscurantist slob—although he remained that—but also a pathetic creature, all the more touching for his monstrousness.

This was one of the features Mona hated most about herself: a terrible susceptibility to sudden attacks of sympathy. It did not matter where she was or what the circumstances: these attacks of sentiment could come on as unexpectedly as a seizure. They were as much physical events as mental, for Mona could feel an itch at her tear ducts and had to focus to restrain herself. At times like this, she felt all but indistinguishable from the person who had elicited her pity. It could be a child or an old man, a vagrant or even some rich celebrity who had brought on the world's scorn with a thoughtless remark; in this case it was Aldo and she could not look at him. She imagined him in his modest apartment, in Elmhurst or Hackensack, eating three TV dinners at a time, held childishly rapt by a golden era

Hollywood romance. What made these episodes especially confusing was they placed Mona for a moment at the exact inverse of her day-to-day relation toward the world—which is to say aloof, unfeeling, estranged.

"Mona," Aldo said, "Still here? What's this new evidence you were talking about?"

Mona took a deep breath. The spell of her sympathy had been broken. "Well, to begin with," she said, "a member of Parr's inner circle *told* me that he was murdered."

"You don't say."

"I do. A representative of Proserpina, Parr's company, came to interview me only a week ago and spilled the beans. He started to deny it afterward, but what's been said can't be unsaid, can it?"

"Hardly," Aldo said, "and for what purpose was this representative of the Proserpina interviewing you?"

"Well, that's a good question. I've been trying to figure it out myself. I don't buy their explanation that they're especially interested in me for their new culture vertical. And to be frank with you—"

"Do be frank."

"To be frank with you, I've gotten the sense that the interview may only have been a cover. I think I was being followed—for what purposes, I can't be sure yet—and that this person, these people—there were two of them, I should have said, Jen and Jon, a bit like Punch and Judy but with tanning lotion and Equinox memberships—only used the interview as a cover when I confronted them and they were forced to explain themselves."

"I see. Highly incriminating. *Well* then, that must have taken some quick thinking on your part."

All Aldo's buffoonery now appeared to have ebbed out, and although he did not give it away in his tone, Mona now got the sense he was toying with her.

"I've also taken a look at the toxicology statements," Mona said, "and I've been conducting my own independent research to check against the autopsy."

The streetlamps outside Aldo's window clicked on. He said nothing. Mona took the moment of silence as a sign she was onto something.

"And as it happens," she continued, "according to my research, the amount of fentanyl recorded in Parr's system is far too much for one individual to have injected with multiple doses, as the autopsy claims. Even someone a lot bigger than Parr ought to have passed out after the initial 12 mg. Which leads me to deduce that someone injected the additional 10 mg into his vein after he had become unconscious."

"May I ask what your independent research consists of?"

"Well," Mona said, "there are various forums on the internet. Mostly Erowid, the DIY pharmacology website, along with a few subreddits. I know a lot of people in your generation are biased against the free exchange of information on the internet—but these forums are filled with trained experts. Of course, not everything you find on a recreational drug use forum is pretty, but the fentanyl boards are highly respectable, and several of the contributors even have MDs."

Silence. Aldo stared at her with his kindly little eyes.

"Mona," he said, "I mean this in all seriousness and with no ill will. I know we've only just met, and I know that I probably don't seem to you like the sort of person who ought to make such a statement, but, have you ever considered looking for a good psychiatrist?"

Mona flinched. The old anger welled up in her.

"Listen," she said, "I'm trying to help you out here. But I can't tell whether you're simply too stupid to do your job correctly, or whether you're intentionally obstructing justice. It should be obvious to a reasonably intelligent twelve-year-old that this death is as fishy as it gets. You have an autopsy that doesn't add up, you have dozens of jealous people who could have wanted him dead, and then you have a ruling of suicide for a man who was too much of an egoist to accept the very *idea* that he might someday cease to be, let alone to do himself in. Anyone who knew Parr at all well—"

"So you did know him well, then?"

"And what if I did, for Christ's sake?"

Aldo smiled and drained the rest of his coffee.

"I'm not sure you knew him as well as you think you do. Parr was many things to many people. You're aware that computational linguistics was not his lone business interest. Some of his other ventures were a little less . . . abstract."

Anxiety took hold of Mona. Something Aldo said did not fit in with the rest.

"I didn't tell you anything about computational linguistics," she said.

"No, you didn't," Aldo said. "Actually, Mona, there are so many things about this case you haven't told me, we could fill a book with them. Whether that's out of innocence or cunning on your part frankly isn't my business. My business is law and order, and making sure that my team doesn't have any amateur gumshoes wandering around where they don't belong. I've got my world, and you've got yours. The two aren't meant to cross."

The two of them sat in silence for a few moments as the air in the musty office seemed somehow to thicken around them, and outside the sun's last evening light dimmed to nothing.

Mona felt a tremor course through her at Aldo's words. It was a distant and dark internal feeling, as though it were taking place somewhere not quite in her own body, but the fear it brought on was piercing and wild. "Christian Rosecrans" had set it loose in her consciousness, but the unease had been dormant in her long before. It seemed to her to emanate not only from the circumstances of Parr's passing but also from her work, her isolation, and the mystery of language itself. A series of unconnected sensations dashed across Mona's mind as she tried to put together the pieces of her investigation and her life. The tram crossing from Roosevelt Island into the city at sunset. Parr's elliptical comments about not seeing her again for a while. The faint hum of midtown below, and the lamplight on Detective Aldo's broad, frowning face.

"Lost in thought again, I see," Aldo said. "I used to get my head stuck in the clouds too, when I was young. But now I've got no time for it. Too many bodies to dig up, meals to put on the table. Here, let me show you the door."

(6)

All was quiet back at Roosevelt Island that evening. No one jogged in gaudy spandex along the Manhattan side of the shoreline, or smoked languidly outside the Riverwalk Bar and Grill. Mona felt exhausted. Whereas on a normal night she would have speed-walked up the escalator from the subway, on this night she let it lift her sore feet along its steady, looping path, and whereas on a normal night she would have happily traipsed along the Queens side of the river up to her home in the Octagon, on this night she simply waited outside the station for the Red Bus. And that, as it turned out, would make all the difference.

The usually reliable bus was twenty-five minutes late (police activity outside Gristedes Supermarket, the driver reported amiably). The only other passenger, a heavy-lidded, Slavic-looking woman with a bald spot, appeared not to have moved from her seat since the fall of the Eastern Bloc. Mona herself might have nodded off at her seat, but apparently the driver was trying to make up time, and raced the bus like a stock car around the island's long oval road before depositing her at her stop.

As she made heavy steps toward her building, Mona felt ready to give up the question of Parr's death. Her meeting with Aldo had sickened her physically. It had been a long time since she'd had to sift through other people's contradictions, their assumptions, their moments of rudeness—to say nothing of their ominously soft voices or wide, fleshy faces. It occurred to Mona that perhaps she had assumed too much. People misspeak all the time. So why had Jon's slip of the tongue made her so certain something evil lurked behind it?

Mona entered the Octagon and immediately spotted Del Park, shooting pool by himself in the front lobby. Del was, at this point in Mona's life, her only real friend—although she would not have enjoyed admitting this fact. The two of them had met when Mona first moved to Roosevelt Island. Around that time Del had retired from his job at a United Nations–related agency (several times he had told Mona which one, but she always managed to forget). Nor did Mona know his age exactly—Del had a kind of ageless, sexless quality that she imagined was often to be found among longtime bureaucrats and middle-managers—but she assumed he had retired a bit ahead of schedule after coming into money. He had, at least, the sunny disposition of a man with independent income, and pointy black boots made with real Italian leather.

But as he no longer had a job, Del needed a truly diverting hobby. At first he took up political outrage—writing long posts on Facebook and splenetic letters to his representatives in Congress. This was the state Mona had found him in when they first became acquaintances. But she immediately sensed that this was not an entirely fulfilling avocation, and tried to guide him toward a different path by closing her eyes for a little longer than could be considered polite whenever he cornered her in the hallway or laundry room or gym and began to monologue about politics. This proving unsuccessful, Mona came up with a different idea. She sussed out that Del had a literary bent and proposed that once a week they hold a "Poetry Hour," in which the two of them could discuss great works of verse. At least it would be better than the inevitable harangues in the hallway. Poetry hour eventually expanded to include great literary works of any kind, and finally expanded even further to include takeout from the good noodle spot on Main Street, a bottle of Malbec apiece, and hours of chitchat on whatever subjects they pleased. Mona was pleased when she discovered that Del was an amateur survivalist who camped out in New York State parks to observe the local flora and fauna. But even with this new subject available, they mostly stuck to books, thereby allowing a genuine affection to develop between them, which might have been impossible, for Mona at least, if there had been too much focus on matters considered personal.

Del spotted Mona and waved her over to the pool table.

"It was a miracle," Del said, "I just hopped the cue clean over the eight ball. Nearly pocketed the five."

"That sounds," Mona said, "like a good thing."

Del had been trying for months now to interest her in their lobby's billiards table, but so far she had managed to resist.

"It was a *miraculous* thing," Del said and frowned. He had a bland hangdog face that was quick to droop with disappointment, but quick too to stretch into a grin. "By the way," he continued, "I didn't realize Shakespeare was such a plagiarist! How come no one has made a stink about that before? You'd think there'd at least be a little Twitter outrage."

For Poetry Hour they had recently been churning through the Bard and his predecessors.

This past week was *The Taming of the Shrew*, and all-but-forgotten George Gascoigne's *Supposes* (itself an adaption from Ariosto's *I Supposi*), from which Shakespeare had lifted the Bianca plot for his own play.

"Why didn't he come up with his own plots, anyway?" Del asked. "Isn't the guy supposed to be a genius?"

Del tried to bank the six off the back wall and into the corner pocket at the opposite end of the table, but he was off by a few degrees.

"You should organize the 'Shakespeare is over' party. I'm sure you could find signatories." Mona said. She did not say, though she was tempted, that plots are the sort of things which are eternal and cannot simply be invented. She was too tired to get into it. The world around her still seemed vaguely menacing.

"I guess he must've just liked the theme," Del said, "of people supposing people are one way, when they turn out to be another. Play of opposites, I guess? Is that why you chose the two plays?"

He handed Mona the pool cue. "Want to shoot?"

The fact was that she had chosen the texts for a deeper, more selfish, and perhaps slightly deranged reason. To wit, from her work with Hildegard, Mona had become convinced that the laws according to which the form and content of poetry progressed were engrained somehow in the fabric of the universe. She intuited that behind the surface of any given work, there lay one long, continuous, not quite decipherable meta-story, unfurling throughout the ages and describing, in its circuitous way, the secret will of the gods (whoever *they* were). This last bit, Mona did realize, was uncomfortably similar to the sort of hunch typically held by paranoid schizophrenics. But she comforted herself with the idea that the truth often resembles madness, that she never saw visions or heard voices, and that she was at least sane enough to be caustically unhappy. In any case, she had begun her task of tracing out English poetic development in the middle, with Shakespeare and his contemporaries—hence *The Taming of the Shrew* and *Supposes*.

Mona took the pool cue and lined up her shot.

"Six ball, side pocket," she said. But before she shot she made a stipulation with herself (this was why Mona disliked bar games such as pool or darts: they forced her back into her own head just when she was most intent on escape) that if she made the shot then she'd give up the question of Parr's death entirely. She pressed the cue stick hard against the bridge between her thumb and index finger, as Del had taught her to do. She crouched to become nearly level with the shot. Concentrate, she told herself, this is for my peace of mind, for all the marbles in my head.

"By the way," Del said, "I know something you don't know that I know."

"Really? Right when I'm lining my shot up?"

"You weren't giving it enough English, anyway. You would have scratched."

Mona lifted up the cue semi-playfully as though to whack Del over the head with it, and for a moment saw real fear in his eyes. She put it down against the table and sighed.

"And what do you know that I don't know you know?"

"I know about your beau who just left. I didn't get much of a look at him, but I hope he's a strapping young fellow."

"What's that?"

"The guy in the khakis and salmon fleece. You know who I'm talking about."

"Del, it's been a long day for me. I assure you I have no idea."

"I'm talking about your lover," Del said. "Or partner, or boy toy, or whatever the kids say these days. The one who was wearing khakis and a salmon fleece. Looked like a professional lacrosse player or something."

Mona laughed. "There are many things uncertain in this world," she said, doing an old Jewish sage by way of vaudeville, "but of this much I am sure. Never shall a man in salmon fleece and khakis enter my bedchamber."

"Then why was he upstairs leaving your room just twenty minutes ago?" Del said. "I saw him when I was coming downstairs. I've seen him around a few times before, too. Really, you surprise me, Mona. There's no need to be bashful."

*

After Mona had led Del upstairs to confirm, again and again, that this man had indeed been seen exiting *Mona's* apartment, and not some other, and after drawing out as many of the details as possible about his appearance and the exact hour of his egress, she borrowed from Del a hunting knife that came with his camping kit, and the two of them tiptoed together into her studio, 12H. They switched on all the lights, they searched every corner, and they checked for all Mona's valuables (an heirloom topaz necklace, and a few first-edition poetry books were the only remotely expensive things she owned). But there was no sign of anyone having been there.

Mona might have chalked up Del's observation to a confusion of time (perhaps he'd noticed this man weeks ago) or place (perhaps Del had noticed him in the main lobby) or sartorial choice (whatever the case, he would not have been wearing a salmon fleece)—but the fact was that a man had not been in Mona's apartment for a very long time. Mona liked to tell herself that this fact was a mere epiphenomenon of her newfound hermeticism. After all, romance did not mesh well with the rejection of the entire outside world. But the truth was that, when it came to matters of the heart, her troubles ran deeper than that.

For some people love and sex were features of existence that seemed to follow naturally from life's premise. Just as it followed naturally from the premise of *fish* that a fish will swim and think nothing of it, the mass of people around Mona seemed to fall in love, fuck, fall out of love, and then begin the process anew—all as naturally as they inhaled and exhaled. And yet for Mona, love and sex were subjects of *thought*. They were to be pondered. In her examinations of these subjects Mona was both the mad professor in a lab coat and the guinea pig. And yet she still remained as far as ever from any intelligent conclusion.

At first Mona had chalked her difficulties up to the fact that she was an intelligent woman. Perhaps, Mona had thought, she intellectualized matters too much. Her mother had been a chess champion, and Mona could not help but approach love and related subjects strategically, with the cunning and coldness of a competitor playing for the win.

But soon Mona learned this strategic-mindedness of hers was not the issue. She had girlfriends in college who would list requirements for suitors as though they were appraising livestock: six foot and above; well-dressed (but not so well-dressed as to outshine the lady); and, above all, normal social skills (filtering out for autism and frightening intensity). Some of them didn't even want their livestock to be healthy: they wanted dad bods, or sleazy facial hair, or drug-addled degeneracy, or various other qualities that left Mona cold. But the point was that they calculated and they calculated successfully. They got the specimens for which they lusted. And Mona got . . . what?

She wasn't quite sure. She got a potpourri of strange experiences—that was the only way she could put it. As a youth she had dreamt of the sort of oversized, rugged, corn-fed boys you simply didn't find in New York City. And then in college she found such boys, and promptly tortured them for being too dumb and humorless for her. One of them, Jim, even threatened to throw himself off a roof. Mona talked him down from that. She promised him he'd find a nice corn-fed girl. Apparently he had never met someone like Mona—who could go from hot to cold in an instant, who could be flirtatiously mean in the Barbara Stanwyck manner, who saw sex as a contest.

Or, more aptly, a combat sport. To Mona, there was always something violent about sex—not just physically but mentally, spiritually. Obviously there were pat psychological explanations for this. But these explanations did not satisfy her for the same reason that materialistic explanations of the joys of literature did not satisfy her: Mona desired these things precisely because there was something in them beyond what could be explained. And like literature, sex was always ultimately unsatisfying. It could not quite scratch the metaphysical itch. Only the *idea* of it could.

But of course that did not prevent Mona from trying, in moments of rashness. It was easy enough to give some strange fantasy a spin. A man on an app, with sunken eyes, who said simply, "you're beautiful," and sent pictures of a well-made bed and heaps of shackles. A tall, athletic, well-rounded hedge fund analyst who begged her to step on him in stilettos. Strangers in dark back rooms smiling darkly, pulling out little baggies of drugs.

It didn't matter. None of this ever scratched the itch for Mona. She got the reputation among her friends for being independent and tough-minded, never fawning over men or too desirous of a partner. But that wasn't quite the truth of the matter, even if it had truth to it. A more accurate statement might have been that she was desperately dependent on a facet of herself that she couldn't quite understand. At least while she was in college, people around her applauded her for this: it was considered a virtue for a smart girl like her not to be duty-bound by a relationship or excessively mushy. But Mona herself could not join them in their applause.

And, in any case, by the time she had reached adulthood, when one was supposed to show one was *capable* of settling down, all that praise for her independence had disappeared.

Once, just after college, she had dated someone she at least felt a kinship with—she might have even said, in a softer moment, that they were one another's best friends. He too was strange, cerebral, had a thorn in his side. They could talk endlessly. They could laugh. But Mona could not escape the evil-seeming pressure of a feeling that there ought to be more for her—something outside the standards of society. Was it to be more like a chaste separation from the world, like that of Hildegard von Bingen? Or was it a sinking deeper into the world's abjectness? Mona could not say. All she knew was that she felt this lack as gnawingly painful, and the pain was always present.

*

"Why didn't you remark that this man in a salmon fleece was leaving an apartment that wasn't his?" Mona asked.

"I didn't want to be nosy," Del said.

"And what did you say to him?"

"'Hi.'"

"And . . . ?"

"And he said 'hi' back. He smiled. He had kind of a sheepish smile. Plain-looking face. Swarthy white guy. Dark hair. Average height. Other than the fleece and khakis, that's all I've got."

Mona told Del to go home and get a head start on the next pairing for Poetry Hour, *Hamlet* and John Marston's *The Malcontent*. Then she fell into bed. She lay there for what felt like hours, letting the scenes from the past few days float through her mind in a dreamlike revue. And all the while, during this state of not-quite-sleep, something nagged at Mona. She felt confident that her apartment had not been burgled, but it seemed to her, inexplicably, to have been violated in some other way. It was an odd feeling, odder still for the insistence with which it forced itself into her mind. It was as though the apartment held a kind of electric charge that had been altered: the component parts of the room's reality had, like a molecule with its swirling electrons, reached its tipping point and had its polarity reversed.

Mona rose from bed and flicked on the light. Here in the bedroom was her dresser, her nightstand, the familiar clothing hung up in her closet. Here in the living area were her big bookshelves and desk. The Riverside Shakespeare open on the kitchen table, humidifier on the floor, old-fashioned coffee maker on the island countertop. All as it should be, bland and familiar. Mona picked up her phone from the counter and unlocked it. No messages. Yet the strings Mona had imagined, earlier that day, to be connecting her to the phone, now seemed to pull at her even more tightly. It was as though it wanted something from her. She paced back and forth unthinkingly, hardly aware of her own movements, washing a few dishes here, turning a lamp on and reading a few lines there—but not putting her mind fully into any of these activities. Then she noticed it. Placed perfectly in the center of the door, just above the peephole, was something that should not have been there. Mona turned on the bright hallway lamp. On the door was a sticker, and on the sticker was a QR code. The code directed her to a web page, which hosted the following short poem:

> Roses are red
> Violets are blue
> Go to the cops again
> And I'll end you.

PART TWO

From the Diary of Avram Parr

March 30, 2015

A paradox: the more extreme my situation, the calmer I feel. When the world around me is in chaos I have the sense of being quite at home. Whereas many supposedly ordinary circumstances feel so malignant to me that I am agitated to the point of murderous rage. In such moments the corporeal elements of life are simply too *present*. Smells, noises, tactile experiences all seem to be conspiring to issue my death sentence. It is as though the *stuff* of the world is rising, rising—to envelop me and suck me down into its primordial filth. I am aware of course that this disposition has features in common with a placement somewhere along what is now known as the autism spectrum; but I refuse to count this disposition of mine as a *disorder*. I refuse to consider it *wrong*. Rather, *they* are wrong who devote their lives rolling in the muck: to their athletic contests and their face makeup and their genital secretions. *They* are wrong, and *I* am right.

A recent example: we acquired this week a new company called Hildegard, and a few members of the board insisted we go out for drinks to "celebrate." I have nothing against alcohol, though I dislike it in excess; nor am I wholly inimical to the practice of revelry. I am capable of taking delight in my actions. But the devil, as always, is in the details.

Jen Rostow rented out a restaurant in Tribeca that people who take interest in restaurants describe as praiseworthy. There were even some interesting people in attendance. Roland Marcos was there, looking only slightly menacing. A couple of bright VCs—Martens and Calloway from Greene Capital—sat quietly in their blindingly white Oxford shirts. I had invited the company's founder—a young woman named Mona Veigh—but she respectfully declined, citing work obligations. Which I must say I appreciated. I like an associate who knows when to decline.

This Mona Veigh created the more promising neural nets for language processing that I've come across. Independent of her project, I began, just for "fun," to see if I could write and categorize a string of all language's component parts. I don't mean grammar, however. I mean motivation: what is a person *doing* when he speaks and expects speech in return from his interlocutor? Sometimes, for instance, he is asking a question in order to ascertain knowledge.

Sometimes he is making a statement to indicate his own high status in a hierarchy of other humans, so as to intimidate rivals or gain power or attract a mate. Sometimes—and perhaps this is the most prevalent category—the sound a man emits from his mouth, though technically consisting of words, is not a speech act at all—but only a spluttering of jibber-jabber meant to allay his own nervousness before the universe's empty silence.

Obviously these musings of mine did not stand me in good stead as I hunkered down for an evening of repartee. Even as I sat there, taking small bites of duck confit, making appropriate facial expressions and speaking appropriate words in response to the general conversation, another part of me was categorizing my interlocutors' speech according to its purpose. As this went on, my despair reached a point near to hysteria. I looked at Jen Rostow's round face, her lips painted mauve, her eyes darting animatedly as she spoke. And yet I could hardly process the words themselves. I could only process what I perceived to be the intention behind the words. In this case: "Look at me. I am sophisticated. I am competent. I am intelligent." A combination, that is, of the *mating* and *hierarchical ascension* speech motivations. I looked at Marcos as he spoke and the same sensation overtook me. His breathy grunts, his elliptical comments: I could see them all branching out from the human motivation decision tree that I might someday invent. Even the way he twisted his lips into a sly smile could be mapped onto the decision tree.

It all felt to me like a version of an experience I have read about called Stendhal Syndrome: an experience some sensitive people have had before works of art. They become overwhelmed by the artwork's supposed beauty and undergo a nervous breakdown. Something similar was now transpiring in me. And yet I found myself overwhelmed not by beauty but by ugliness, veniality, hypocrisy, deceit. By the insurmountable gap between the spoken word and what the spoken word was meant to convey. Not one person at the table spoke simply in order to share information with the other. No one said precisely what he meant. I felt simultaneously sick and godlike in my ability and willingness to see through the essence of the situation.

I rose from the table and made some barely audible excuse. I stepped out onto the street.

The streetlamps seemed to me especially bright, and the smell of summer garbage especially nauseating; but the absence of human voices was simply divine. I fell to my knees and vomited into the gutter. The semi-digested duck confit before me seemed to me similar to those semi-digested thoughts that had emerged from my interlocutors in the form of words. I felt tremendous. I felt purged. I do not believe in God, but if I did I would have thanked Him for emptiness, for the absence of vile nonsense. I will never allow myself to be submerged again in this muck. I will speak only what is necessary, to whom it is necessary. And I will consider how best to implement the potential energy of what I have discovered.

(7)

The digital threat that had been pinned to Mona's wall was, in its form at least, not unfamiliar: she had a history with QR codes. Just out of college, when Hildegard was still but a twinkle in her eye, Mona had amused herself by creating her own personal QR codes and posting them throughout the city. At first Mona would post stickers with codes that led to pages displaying her favorite poems. Then she got truly ambitious and posted codes that contained only bits and pieces of poems she admired, and which required the intrepid scanner to find the complementary codes posted on nearby street corners in order to solve the puzzle. Mona mined the analytics data of the pages and found that a few people had in fact followed her trail successfully.

Soon enough Mona tired of these hijinks, and these days it exhausted her even to think of the high-spiritedness it had taken to paste the codes on random street corners. But for several years afterward she had remained fond of using QR codes in her personal life. The code leading to "My Last Duchess," for instance, was stuck beside an eighteenth-century oil painting of a weatherworn lady aristocrat that Mona had bought on the cheap, and the one leading to Childe Harold's stanzas on Lake Geneva's sublimity was stuck next to her bath. So when Parr bought Hildegard, Mona used QR codes for a very special purpose: as a means by which to exploit a bizarre clause her boss had drawn up in the contract between them.

The situation was this: while Parr had allowed Mona to keep her codebase private, he stipulated that she was free to encrypt her work in whatever way she pleased, while he was free to attempt at his leisure to breach her defenses. In Parr, there was much of the old hacker ethos—which saw software as a game more than anything else, even if the game turned out to be played for billions of dollars. Like the great hackers of yore (back in the day, *hacker* was not a pejorative), Parr cared about proving one's mettle above all else, and he brought that spirit to his company in various sly ways.

Mona, however, was up for the challenge. It occurred to her that there was only one domain where she might outwit her opponent: physical reality; or, to use the term Parr preferred, *meatspace*. Mona was free to use whatever sort of encryption she liked, but that method did not need to be entirely digital.

Hence, the QR codes. Mona created a trail of them that would lead back to the sacred house of Hildegard. They had to be scanned in a specific order, which Mona would change every few months or so, and once that had been done the user would be given a link to the repository where Hildegard's code lived and breathed. Mona was of course aware of the danger that these QR code stickers might be removed or damaged. But this was pretty easily worked around. Mona had laminated them and attached a miniature GPS tracker to the back of each. Then she set her program so that if the code moved outside a 500-foot radius of wherever she had placed it, then it would self-destruct, as it were, and be eliminated from the string of QR codes that had to be scanned before Hildegard was revealed. So far none of them had been damaged or removed.

One of them had been scanned, however. This took place just a month or so before Parr died: the scan corresponded to a code Mona had placed on a pedestal at Four Freedoms Park, on the northern end of Roosevelt Island. Once scanned, the code was programmed to send a randomly generated Hildegard poem to Mona's email address. Mona eventually came to regard it as a mere accident—perhaps some tween at the park hoping the code would lead to a free video game download—though Mona nearly jumped out of her seat at the public library when she first saw the email. The poem that had been generated, titled "Hildegard's Advice to Her Book," was a mock-*l'envoi*, from the author to the product of his or her authorship, as in Chaucer's farewell to *Troilus and Criseyde* ("Go, litel boke, go litel myne tragedye...") or Edmund Spenser's epilogue to *The Shepheardes Calendar*. Mona read the poem and merely felt sad. It pained her to see Hildegard's work again, after so long a hiatus. She decided not to look at any other poems that might crop up if more QR codes were scanned. Mona set them to filter straight into her spam folder.

The rest of the QR codes were scattered throughout the city, with a heavy emphasis on Roosevelt Island. One, for instance, was in Del's apartment, stuck surreptitiously to the bottom of his seldom-used blender. Another was under a bench by the Tech campus. Farther afield, she had placed one in the ladies' toilets of her favorite bakery in the financial district, one underneath a ceiling panel of Hildegard's old office building, and one on the underside of a metal slide at a jungle gym she'd frequented as a child in Queens.

The final code was as close to home as could be. Inside Mona's big *Norton Anthology of English Poetry, Vol. 2*, there was a favorite of hers, Algernon Swinburne's "Hymn to Proserpine." The poem itself was a euphonious ode to that death goddess of the title, whom Swinburne believed would soon return to her former glory. And it was, above all, an ode to the idea of death as the greatest of all transcendent powers, as an eternal sleep not to be interrupted by some crummy pseudo-halcyon afterlife. Mona put the sticker on the bottom corner of the page beside the next-to-last lines of the poem, which read:

Thou art more than the Gods who number the days of our temporal breath;
Let these give labour and slumber; but thou, Proserpina, death.
Therefore now at thy feet I abide for a season in silence. I know
I shall die as my fathers died, and sleep as they sleep; even so.

Mona grimaced at the irony that these lines should be associated with Parr, that striver after perpetual life. She read the poem once more, lingering over its voluptuous melancholy. Then she turned the page and did not look back.

*

First thing, after rising from a sleepless night, Mona texted Natalie to let her know they needed to meet as soon as possible. It was a brilliant morning, the skyscrapers across the river all reflecting distortions of one another, those distortions all shifting as clouds passed by and the sun traveled its course. Mona shielded her eyes with her hand as she stepped out into the day, and beat a steady path toward the middle of the island where she could catch the tram. She was trying hard as she could to keep her anxiety at bay, at least until she could speak to Natalie. She pulled her Metrocard from her bag, which now also contained the knife Del had lent her, and swiped her way through to board the tram.

As usual, a couple of children scurried up to the front of the tramcar to better their view, as usual an old derelict dozed imperturbably on the car's back bench, and as usual Mona's stomach dropped as the tram ascended: she closed her eyes for a few moments to gather herself and shut out the sun. But when she opened them she still felt queasy. Typically Mona's vertigo on the tram would resolve itself after the first lurch skyward. But this afternoon every inch of movement along the steel cables' arc seemed to renew her dizziness, her sense of being somewhere she ought not to be. The car swayed in the wind as it reached its peak over the river. There wasn't supposed to be turbulence on the tram, was there? Mona, at least, had never experienced it before. But no one in the car seemed to notice, except for a child up front, who shouted "whoa" and made an exaggerated display of losing his balance. Mona did what she often did in moments of distress: she recited poetry to herself in her head.

"I to my perils of cheat and charmer," she mouthed, "came clad in armor by stars divine. Hope lies to mortals and most believe her—"

The car swayed again. This time several of her fellow passengers looked around at one another for confirmation of the jolt and smiled weakly to show each other that they were not truly worried.

"—But man's deceiver was never mine. My thoughts of others were light and fleeting—"

This manner of warding off the world had begun in Mona's childhood. Whenever her mother was clanking dishes angrily or shouting at the television, she would put in a pair of earplugs—bought in bulk at the CVS on Northern and 89th for just this purpose—and pull out her two-volume *Norton Anthology of Literature*. This tended to be effective: usually the shouting would last no more than half an hour or so, and the clanking of dishes would end when her mother got sloshed enough to lie down, leaving a blessed period of respite. (As the tramcar descended into the glare of the city, it rocked once more, this time so dramatically that all the standing passengers had to shift their footing, and even the imperturbable old man in the back awakened with a scowl.)

"Of lovers' meetings, or luck, or fame," Mona whispered.

That it had been a wretched childhood was not something Mona dwelled on or even admitted into the narrative she had of herself. And oddly enough, she didn't feel angry or sad when she thought about it. Intellectually, it occurred to her that it might have been better to have known her father, or a mother who had not been a drunk, but on the other hand so many had it so much worse, and she didn't see what good grieving over the past would do her. What she felt instead was a numbness, a block—as though her past were something rather unpleasant and tawdry that had happened to someone else. Or as though it were some depressing movie, a grim parable set in medieval Scandinavia, say, that she'd watched once years ago but had mostly forgotten. Certain images stayed with her— the interminable gray expanse of the Queens cemetery where Mona visited her father's grave as a girl, her mother's empty magnums of Chianti hidden in the dumbwaiter till recycle day—but the recollections did not add up to any emotion in her. They had come and gone like flashes on a screen. They were fundamentally unreal.

Mona finished the poem in her head: "Mine were of trouble, and mine were steady, so I was ready when trouble came."

The tramcar touched down softly on Manhattan's East Side, where the unfeeling crowd went briskly on about its business.

*

Mona had not visited Hildegard's old office building since Parr died. Presumably the space now housed some other company's offices, though she had no idea which. It was an open-plan space—this was the trend at the time—which Mona had loathed. Anyone on her team could sidle up to her for a question at any hour of the day. There was nowhere to hide. In the wide, brightly lit room she had felt like Prometheus punished, splayed open for all to see, and continually pecked at.

"Now you will be able to collaborate," Parr said when he first showed it to her.

Previously Hildegard had been run out of her cubbyhole studio in the Financial District. And sometimes the bakery on Church where they never ran out of almond croissants. Never before had Mona had a real team.

"What if I don't know *how* to collaborate," Mona said.

"It is not so very difficult. You'll learn."

"I can't imagine *you* do much collaboration."

"On the contrary," Parr said. "I collaborate all the time. Collaboration is merely using someone else's skill stack to further your own goals. Why, come to think of it, I am collaborating with you right now."

"That sounds more like parasitism."

"Not in the least. I offer something to my collaborators that is far greater than what I take from them. Do you know what that is?"

"Money."

"Vision," Parr said. "I provide my collaborators with vision. A vision for how all the pieces fit together, so that the whole is greater than the sum of its parts. That, and yes, money too. Money is a given."

The subordinate employees Parr had given Mona once she'd become part of the Proserpina team had also believed in Parr's vision. This was a bright and rosy vision, which gave a picture of the future as a place of peace and good cheer. Basically, the people Parr had assigned to Mona were techno-optimists. They believed there was no feature of human suffering that technology could not solve. They had keen ideas about brilliant, talking robots who could comfort or advise their human interlocutors, and they believed that working on Hildegard might point them in the right direction.

"Think about it," one of them said to Mona one morning while she was sitting on the office beanbag, "in the future, AI could be able to shoot a movie or write a whole book personalized for *you*. It could contain all your favorite themes, in just your favorite style. It could know your preferences better than you do."

"Be careful what you wish for," Mona said. "What the AI knows about you might not be the same as what you know about yourself. You might not be so pleased to find out your own preferences."

"What do you mean?" the employee said, "if they're your preferences, then you like them."

The young man had a fair point, of course. They always had fair points. Yet all their fair points did not add up to anything convincing. One crucial element was always left out. And that was the human capacity for self-sabotage, the absolute unwillingness of the species to let anything be absolutely perfect. Mona tried to imagine a world in which artificially intelligent machines farmed all the food humans needed, cured all human diseases, and provided all human pleasures. The thought was sickening. Not because she had any particular horror of a Terminator-style uprising, or of multitalented sex robots. Rather, because the idea of contentment itself sickened her. Mona knew that displeasure, even chaos, was necessary for what she held most dear in life.

*

Mona pushed through her old building's revolving doors and was greeted by a swell of cold air. Alex, the doorman, did not notice her immediately. She could see from the reflection against the glass wall behind him that he was playing a knock-off version of Candy Crush on his phone. As Mona shuffled her feet, he swiveled toward her in his chair and scrunched up his eyes.

"Back for more?" he said, as though only a week, not six months, had passed. "You must be a real glutton for punishment."

Mona rejoiced to see his long, pockmarked face. She had never learned much about his life—though for some reason she'd got it into her head that he was from the Balkans—and she'd never said much of substance to him, either. And yet they'd developed that affinity common among New Yorkers who interact on a daily basis: a skillful exchange of comments on the weather, a hearty injunction to have a good weekend, all tempered by a shared sense of irony toward the whole charade of forced idle conversation, and even, perhaps, toward one another's very existence. "I just couldn't get enough. How's tricks? The kids, the wife?" Mona had no idea whether Alex actually had kids or a wife. This was just their little routine.

"Oh, tip-top shape," he said, "and for you how's tricks? The kids, the hubby?"

"They're grand," Mona said, "just grand."

He pressed a button to retract the metal pincers of the computerized gate, and Mona crossed the lobby to the elevator bay. Up she went to floor seven. Mona could never quite believe that elevators actually ascended. It felt to her more like teleportation, preceded by motion sickness. The nimbus around the button indicating the seventh floor faded away, and Mona stepped out of the car into her past.

Except that the space had been successfully infiltrated by the present: the walls had been painted, and the door to Hildegard's old office, 706, now bore a bronze plaque for "Ross & Parino." Mona tried the door. Locked. There were no voices to indicate anyone inside. Perhaps Ross &

Parino was a consulting firm that only worked odd hours. She remembered another, lesser-known entrance on the opposite side of the U-shaped corridor and began to make her way across the linoleum. She did not know how, but she felt certain that the second door would be unlocked. And, even stranger, she felt sure that whatever she found inside would be of interest to her.

Mona turned the corner and began to walk along the long central base of the corridor's *U* shape. But she had not got halfway toward the end of it when she heard footsteps behind her. The steps echoed from around the bend from which she had just come. She felt a jolt of fear threatening to overwhelm her—not so much in her mind, but viscerally, as a shiver along the nape of the neck and a weakness in her legs. The footsteps were steady, purposeful. Mona remembered a stairwell at the next bend and made up her mind to escape down it. As the steps came closer, she exhorted herself not to look back. Then she looked back. It was a large man in a dark suit.

"Excuse me, ma'am," he said, "may I have a word with you?"

He spoke calmly and firmly. The tone was neither polite nor rude. Mona's first instincts were to punch him, or to run. Could this be the man in the salmon fleece? He didn't look like the sort of man who would wear a salmon fleece, but one could never be sure. Mona unzipped her bag to search for the knife, then turned again to size him up. About a foot taller than her, broad shoulders. Blank, inscrutable face.

"No," Mona said, "I'm afraid you can't."

She hurried toward the stairwell. His footsteps echoed behind hers. Run, she told herself. But somehow she could not run. Mona reached the door to the stairwell and grasped the handle. It would not open. The man in the suit was now directly behind her. She pressed all her weight against the door, but it was no use. Why wouldn't it open? It was as though she were stuck in a bad dream. Mona felt the sleek handle of the knife in her bag. She turned to the man, thrust the knife from the bag and unlocked its blade.

"Stay back!" she said.

"It's a pull door," he said, "would you do me a favor and put that thing away? Assaulting a government official will land you thirty to life." He pulled out a badge from his pocket and lifted up the hem of his suitcoat to reveal a pistol. "I was hoping we could be a little more discreet. There are more cameras in here than in Sing Sing. I'm Special Agent Marcos. What do you say we take the elevator instead?"

(8)

"I want," Marcos said, "for this to be taken as much as possible in the spirit of a casual chat. No charges are being pressed. But we need to establish a few facts. I'm speaking, you may have guessed, about your involvement in the case of Avram Parr."

They sat down on ungainly cement seats in an isolated area of a corporate park on 47th. In the waning afternoon light Mona was able to give Marcos a proper look up and down. He was large and handsome in a jowly, simian sort of way. Medium-length dark hair pomaded and parted to the side, narrow brown eyes, soft fleshy lips. His dark suit was sufficiently FBI-esque, as were his elegant black dress shoes. The only thing Mona found to be incongruous was a hemp bracelet around his right wrist. She willed herself to sit very upright and assume a calm demeanor, while drops of cold sweat trickled down the nape of her neck. How had this man, she wondered, known immediately to question her about Parr?

"I don't know what you're talking about," Mona said weakly.

"I can see in your face that you're not stupid, so it won't help to pretend to be. Perhaps you'd like to start by informing me what you were doing snooping around 340 Madison."

Mona wiped the sweat from her neck. She had no intention of speaking openly until she understood what she was dealing with.

"I don't suppose you would accept," Mona said, "that I just happened across it on my afternoon stroll."

"Afraid not. Alex has already given me your basic information, including the fact that you used to work there?"

"*Alex* did?"

"I've had this office building locked down for months now, and I paid off Alex to let me know if anyone out of the ordinary shows up. He was good to his word."

"That sneaky Balkan bastard," Mona said. "So he's not even working the door?"

"Alex is from Latvia, actually. And he's working the door in the sense that his job is to sit near it. But otherwise, no. These offices are empty."

"Then what's Ross & Parino? That name was on the door to my old workspace." Marcos gave no answer, and the two of them sat for a moment in silence. Midtown, brimming with human drama at midday, began at this hour to drain of its coherence: the managerial class shuffled home, shouting the day's last items of jargon into their devices, trapezoidal shadows stretched across soulless pedestrian plazas, and the lights of emptying towers clicked on.

"I fear," Marcos said, "that we may have got off on the wrong foot. I should explain to you that your old office building has been broken into several times since Parr's lease ended. Thus my assignment. It doesn't seem likely that you're the perpetrator, but it would make things easier on me if you tell me what you were doing here. We may be able to help each other."

"So this isn't an official questioning in any way, shape or form?"

"Couldn't be less official," Marcos said, "Avram Parr was a friend of mine. I'm hoping you might be a friend, too."

Mona gave a version of her story, leaving out certain sensitive details, such as her acquaintance with Natalie and the threatening QR code that had been stuck to her door. After her encounter with Detective Aldo, she was not eager to reveal just how far she had already traveled down this road of conspiracy. Marcos waited a long while before responding to her.

Mona couldn't tell whether he was going over her story for holes, or merely trying to give her the impression that he was deep in thought. Either way, he scratched his chin. It was a large, dimpled chin, with a hint of grainy stubble.

"According to your story," Marcos said, "it's been close to a year since your company dissolved. What exactly have you been up to since then?"

"Sitting at home, reading poetry, mostly."

"*Poetry*? What for?"

It was making Mona sicker and sicker, having to answer versions of this question. At first it was because she didn't feel she had the energy or the patience to explain why it was that poetry mattered to her—why it was that anything should matter to anyone independent of its utility, of its capacity to create income or make the world more efficient. But now the question sickened her because she was not sure she could give a sound answer even to herself. And without that self-justification, what did she have left?

"I have no major problem with poetry," Marcos offered, once it became apparent Mona was not going to answer, "but I prefer nonfiction. With poetry, I always wondered, why not just come out and say the thing?"

"But what's the *thing*?" Mona asked.

"Well that's exactly what the two of us are going to find out."

*

The park closed at dusk and the two of them began to walk. Mona had been obsessively checking her phone since the morning for an update from Natalie and now sent a follow-up message, trying not to sound pushy or desperate. Finally Natalie responded. She said she wasn't available until 10:00 p.m. that night.

"What do you say we drop in somewhere for a drink?" Marcos asked.

It took a few extra paces down the avenue before Mona could process his question. They were approaching Grand Central from its rear, and the hordes of commuters bustling around 35th seemed to her uncomfortably like extras on a movie set. Bald man shouting about money into Bluetooth, check. Aged stately doyenne, check. Large tourist family, all in hoodies emblazoned with the logo of the local team, check. Mona felt at this moment that she had to devote extra energy to making certain that she stayed grounded in reality. Everything in her field of vision, including the besuited man swinging his arms beside her, read to her as inscrutable, jumbled, overly familiar and yet outside the "everyday" version of life she once might have known.

"You wouldn't say it's out of order for a federal officer to be taking a potential suspect out for a drink?"

"Well," Marcos said, "about the federal officer thing."

"Yes. About the federal officer thing."

"For five years I really *was* a fed. The problem is, most of what government spooks are doing these days is just intercepting one another's laundry lists. A fifteen-year-old can get as much intel working from his mom's basement in Minsk as a seasoned government professional can. So three years ago I left the State for Osiris, a private integrative intelligence firm, and a year and a half ago Parr hired us out to keep an eye on his properties. I had to lie to get you to your attention. You weren't safe wandering around that building. You understand, don't you?"

Mona understood at least the fact that she had gone too deep down the rabbit hole to try to escape by climbing out. She was going to have to keep digging, and hope that she might emerge, however disoriented, on the other side. And that meant getting as much information as she could from whomever came her way. So she got into a black Lexus with Marcos and they rode haltingly through rush-hour traffic toward the low orange sun. It was only once they'd got to the West Side Highway that Mona realized it was not an Uber but a private car. All Mona could see of the driver was a pale, girthy neck, the folds of which vibrated as the car accelerated.

"Where are we going?" she asked, but neither Marcos nor the driver spoke. Only at the next stoplight did Marcos say softly:

"Hope you like surprises."

"Not really."

He did not turn to her but faced straight ahead, tapping his fingers on his knees as though he were playing an invisible piano. Now that he had abandoned the pretense of being a Fed, Marcos's comportment loosened up, and he leaned back in his seat, resting his thick arms on the seat back, and spreading his legs wide. With the easy confidence of a salesman, Marcos began to tell stories, still not looking at Mona, only tilting his face toward her occasionally to see if she had reacted to a particular witticism. His aftershave smelled of almonds, sugar, chlorine, and sweat. His jawline was sharp and his cheek was smooth. Mona scooched her body away from him and rolled her window down, placing her open palm against the current of air as they sped down the west side past the glittering glass constructions of Hudson Yards. From the corner of her eye Mona could see Marcos smile as though all this were exactly according to plan. He reached the end of a story about his first year with the Feds, in which they'd discovered that the cast of a crippled man departing from Guatemala was made partly of plaster and partly of cocaine, and gave a long pause, waiting, it seemed, for the light to change from red to green, before he started to tell the story of how he'd first met Avram Parr.

*

"I want you to know that I have powerful enemies."

This was what Parr said as soon as Marcos stepped through the private elevator doors into Parr's Gramercy Park duplex.

"Excellent apartment," Marcos said, "have you been here long?"

"My enemies are powerful," Parr continued without acknowledging the question, "but they are not especially intelligent. The positive side of their not being especially intelligent is that they can be defeated. The negative side is that when they are defeated, they won't know it. They won't know when to quit. In fact, from a certain perspective, they were defeated before they even began. They were defeated by the dawning of an age that rendered them obsolete."

"Should I sit? Or just stand here in the entryway?"

"Because my enemies are not especially intelligent and because their cause is so hopeless, they are dangerous. They are like a petulant child who would set the whole world aflame, if he had the power, because his parents have taken away a favorite toy."

Marcos took the liberty of sitting down on Parr's couch. It was a black leather two-seater. "That seems to me," Marcos said, "to be taking a rather dark view of crying children."

"Look at one the next time you see one," Parr said, "look at their glowing little angry eyes."

Parr then, standing over Marcos, looked intently into *his* eyes, as if to provide an example for how Marcos ought to inspect the eyes of an upset toddler.

"And so my enemies," Parr continued, "must be placated. They must not know how obsolete they have become. Like children, they must be comforted."

"You want me to send them flowers?"

"What I want you to do," Parr said, "is to soften the blow of my existence. Make Proserpina look like something they can contain. Make my enterprises look less threatening. Make me look—normal."

Marcos did not interject to say just how tall an order that last request would be. Instead he brought up money. Parr offered him a salary at the upper limits of what might be expected, Marcos immediately accepted, and they stayed up most of the night talking strategy. To celebrate their partnership, Parr offered the full range of his cordials: Soylent, kombucha, a pill bottle of Nuvigil, and cerebrolycin, which was apparently an injectable form of pig brains that worked as a nootropic and was legal in Russia. Marcos thought this was meant to be at least partly humorous but it was not. So he went out for a handle of vodka and a case of Red Bull. They talked about Osiris Integrative's *Six-Pronged Strategy of Influence*. This consisted of

1. Positive Propaganda
2. Misdirection
3. Opposition Research
4. Disinformation
5. Threats of Force
6. Use of Force

"The sixth prong is seldom necessary," Marcos said, "but it was good to have it available: 'speak softly but carry a big stick,' as the saying goes."

Parr sat motionless and attentive as Marcos explained the prongs in fastidious detail.

Marcos had emptied the full case of Red Bull by the time dawn spread through Parr's penthouse like a disinfectant, though he had managed to kill only half of the handle of vodka. Parr was so pleased by their partnership that Marcos convinced him to take a few shots, teetotaler though he was.

"Now will you tell me," Marcos said, hoping the alcohol might bring on at least a hint of chumminess, "whether you've been in this apartment long?"

"I truly don't remember. I do not to take much notice of my immediate surroundings. Before I moved to New York full-time I would stay in hotels. Eventually I told my assistant to purchase a conveniently located and noiseless apartment. If I were to estimate, I would say this occurred three and a half years ago."

"Your assistant sure didn't spare any expense."

"Now that you draw my attention to it," Parr said, "I rather despise it. To have an expensive apartment is to hang a target around your neck. That's the last thing I need."

"Why not enjoy yourself a little?" Marcos said. He was sprawled on the leather couch and was beginning to doze. "You've earned the right to, at least."

"Enjoyment," Parr said, "is not to my taste. Neither is ostentation. One purchases nice things simply out of habit when one is wealthy. But in the end, the nice things only get in the way. And turn one into the enemy of people who do not have nice things but desire them."

From the east-facing windows Marcos could see the sun over the river as it began to singe the city with purple and gold. From this vantage the land below no longer seemed like New York—but rather, like a strange, resplendent island nation that had grown out of apocalyptic fire. Marcos imagined himself as the king of it as he fell asleep on the couch, looking down on the hordes from the turret of a castle.

A few hours later he was awakened by a hard prod on the shoulder from Parr. "Get up," he said, "We must leave."

Marcos opened his eyes to the unpleasant sight of Parr already in jacket and boots, looming over him and glancing continually at his smart watch.

"Going on a trip?" Marcos said.

"No. The realtors will be here soon. While you were sleeping, I sold the place."

*

The car pulled up to what Marcos called his favorite spot downtown. It was, by appearances, an old punk bar. In his teens, Marcos said, in the early nineties, he had come here just about every night. Yet on this night the punks were nowhere to be found. Nor had any new clientele come to replace them. The walls were graffitied, the toneless music was loud, but the place was deserted. One of the figures spray-painted on the wall was a monstrous cartoon character, consisting of two conjoined faces. The brow and forehead of one face served as the jaw of the second face, which was stacked totem-wise on top of it. Mona found the image uncommonly disturbing. As she stared at it she was suddenly assailed by a bizarre sense that the image was alive in some very real way, chumming it up with a whole invisible horde of wall-bound grotesqueries—and that, somehow, the punks of yore had been only the medium through which these chaotic images, including spirals, silhouettes, and de Kooning-style splats, had come into existence. Now these grotesqueries on the wall were the building's true occupants. Mona shook herself awake from her reverie.

"What did Parr mean his enemies had to be *placated*?" she asked.

"He wanted them to feel like they had things under control. He funded fact-checking organizations and vaguely anti-corporate nonprofits to keep them under his watch. Meanwhile he was paying off the people who really mattered."

"Paying them off for what?"

"That I never learned. I was just the muscle, you know."

Marcos looked like an oversized hang-dog as he shook his head and frowned, awkwardly rearranging his large body in the narrow wooden booth in order to point to his bicep.

"I'm going to go out on a limb and trust you," Mona said.

She took out her phone and showed Marcos the threatening poem that had been left for her last night.

"Got any ideas who might have written this," Mona said, "even if you *are* only the muscle? They broke into my apartment too."

Marcos read the poem and then cast his gaze upward, remaining thoughtful for a moment, as though he were receiving wisdom directly from the cacophonous music sounding out from the speakers above.

"What did you say was the name of the detective you talked to?"

"I didn't. But his name was Aldo."

"And you said he seemed to know more about you than he really should have?"

For a moment the music stopped. Mona could hear her heart pound as she waited for the shrieking and the cymbals to recommence.

"You're saying the New York City Police Department wrote me a note threatening me not to go to the New York City Police Department?"

"Think a minute. It accomplishes two goals at once: getting you out of their hair while simultaneously placing the blame for Parr's death somewhere else."

"Because the *police* killed Avram Parr?"

"Not necessarily the cops themselves. Maybe all they did was look the other way while a hired gun took him out. Parr wasn't kidding when he said he had powerful enemies. People in high places, maybe higher than we know about. Call it the global order, call it what you want. The people who comprise it are hardly aware of it—they're just playing their roles according to some far out logic that's beyond even their understanding. They'd blow the world up and have us start all over again from single-celled organisms before they let go of the position they've got. The force they obey is stronger than any of us and any of us can be sacrificed to it."

Mona downed her drink. She was clasping her hands together so hard that her knuckles had turned white. She disliked the conspiratorial tone of Marcos's speech. Yet she recognized in it a twisted version of her own deepest fear: that the world of what she held most dear was being slowly eroded by an inexorable force she could not put her finger on. She began to feel a tension headache—more like a deep tingling than an ache—build up in the space between her eyes, as the music over the speakers reached an ugly crescendo.

"You all right?"

"Could we go somewhere else? Say, anywhere, anywhere at all that's not here?"

They paid and moved to a bench on the western edge of Tompkins Square. The veiny leaves of the gingkoes above them shone yellow from the streetlamps. Beyond, little crowds smoked and cavorted along the dark expanse of Avenue A. Marcos, it turned out, had a hip-pocket flask, and he brought out a boxy, complicated-looking vape, the size of deodorant stick, to go along with it.

"How can it be," Mona asked, "that I'm talking to someone who smokes one of those things?"

"Perhaps because I'm a charming, handsome spy, who's also a great listener."

"Or perhaps," Mona said, "it's because I've got no one else to talk to."

Marcos took a drag from his machine. The smoke unfurled slowly, tracing a spiral up above Mona's head. He waved it away apologetically, before letting his hand rest for a moment on her elbow.

"What's more interesting to me," Marcos said, slowly removing his hand, "is how you got to be such a cynic."

"*That*," Mona said, "could take a whole lifetime to tell."

"Did I mention I'm a great listener?"

Mona rolled her eyes at him. But before she knew it, the words began to spill from her mouth.

(9)

Mona's father had died when she was eight years old: not tragically or heroically, but at least stubbornly, of lung cancer, smoking a pack a day of Marlboro Reds till the end. That was the way Mona's mother told it, and from her faint memories of the man Mona had no difficulty believing it. She recalled, with the weird vividness of a memory constructed partly from events for which one is not actually present, that he had the air of a man peculiarly resigned to fate, and peculiarly certain that fate had an evil intent. Mona could even recall intuiting this quality of his from the contours of his sallow, equine face. As a teenager it occurred to her to question the moral uprightness of a man with a young child who blithely hastens his own death, but when she said this to her mother, she responded that the cancer was far enough along when they discovered it that he had no chance no matter what he did. It made sense to Mona, and she didn't fault him for it. It would be *nice* to believe that if a man is told he's got only a few months to live, he'll resolve to change his life, Rilke-like, and make those last months count. And yet, she reasoned to herself, the idea of death is so alien to a person's everyday conception of the world that the most likely reaction would be to keep doing what one has always done, fixing breakfast, going over expenses, grounding oneself in "reality"—until that moment when the heart stops, and last week's tax preparation, tomorrow's breakfast, and today's hopes become less real than the most outlandish fiction.

Long before her husband's death, Mona's mother had been an odd duck. She was also brilliant—or at least she had been once. For although she was still cagey and scrupulously devoted to a few intellectual tasks, it was Mona's opinion that her brilliance had deteriorated, along with her once-lustrous black hair and willingness to socialize with other humans. Her name was Valentina, and that was what Mona thought of her as these days—not *Mom*. She had met Mona's father in that most old-fashioned of ways: he approached on the street, sensing intrigue from her looks and her gait. And his premonition was confirmed when he learned that the young woman he had just stopped and stammered at as she strolled down Riverside was a Romanian physicist and former chess prodigy. Mona could imagine her mother putting it just like that: "Hello, my name is Valentina. I am a physicist and former chess prodigy."

That in itself probably would have been enough for Mona's father, a bland-looking transplant to the city from South Bend, Indiana. Nor did it hurt that Valentina was tall and elegant, with darting, ironical eyes. She was doing postdoc research then at Columbia on a statistical model of the multiverse theory. She stopped her research when Mona was born, started up again five years later, then stopped permanently when Mona's father died. But she never stopped teaching and gave the same dry and difficult Intro to Astrophysics course every semester at CUNY Queens. But, later in life, most of her time was devoted to two occupations, each of which was holy to her in its own way: drinking and chess.

The boozing began soon after Mona's father had died. The chess madness had always been there—Mona's mother had earned her FIDE Master and Woman Grandmaster titles at the age of twenty—but now it turned evil, like a vine strangling the trunk of its host. In the years that Mona was witness to, it seemed to bring her no joy, and Valentina was too old now to improve. Yet she played the computer for hours at a time with her jaw clenched, and went out to local tournaments and complained to the arbiters about the lights that were always too bright above her. One of those times an opponent of hers returned the favor by complaining that

Valentina's alarming vodka breath gave her an unfair advantage. The game ended in a draw.

Beginning in early adolescence Mona had felt competitive with her enigmatic and intelligent mother. She imagined this was not uncommon among children of people with strong personalities, but Mona's loss of her father, and her own headstrong nature, made the situation more pronounced. Plus there was the fact that Valentina had been too cold—too much the me-against-the-world Eastern European immigrant to ever be especially motherly. Mona never knew whether Valentina resented having to raise a child alone, whether she disliked that Mona was a reminder of the man she had lost, or whether her aloofness and bitterness were simply part of her personality.

But by the time Mona was old enough to formulate this question, she was less interested in understanding than in combatting this dour roommate out of whose womb she had emerged. She began with defense. Mona bought a dead bolt for her door with summer job money and made sure to be as taciturn as possible whenever she had to come out from behind it for sustenance or its eventual disposal. Valentina made sure to act a little aggrieved, but it was evident she welcomed this bit of antagonism: just as some people are born for love or sport or madness, others are born for war. It was only when Valentina threatened one evening, late into a magnum of chianti, to clear out Mona's poetry books while Mona was at school because the apartment was "feeling a touch cramped" and she didn't like to feel that some eighteenth-century tome was continually in danger of falling on her head, that Mona had to go on the offensive. Mona knew the threat came purely from spite. (She had recently disinterred one of her mother's bottles from deep in the living room bookshelf and placed it provocatively on the kitchen counter.) But she wasn't willing to wait and find out. She said that if any of those books went missing, she'd call social services, and then leave and live on the street, and Valentina knew that her daughter was just wild and stubborn enough to do it.

Valentina, after all, wasn't *that* malicious. More than anything, Mona grew to see her as sad. The old woman would always sit at the same spot when Mona returned home, sipping the third or fourth glass of the evening, pale green eyes affixed to the chessboard where she'd play out openings. Mona herself had shown promise as a kid, but never took to the game competitively. Occasionally, however, she'd get a match in with her mother when pity overpowered antipathy, and would be summarily trounced. And it was these occasional games, Mona realized now, that had led without her knowing it to computer science: Deep Blue had taken down Kasparov not even a decade ago, and it was clear that computers, not humans, were the future of chess. It tickled Mona to know that this world of sixty-four black and white squares into which her mother had retreated was revealing itself to be a place where living, breathing people were not ultimately needed. Between the computer and Valentina, the computer could always be the more unfeeling. So Mona found a way, through programming, to beat her mother at her own game. And yet she knew this was something more than pure vengeance on her own part. It occurred to her these days, and the thought was equal parts beautiful and terrifying, that all strong emotions, no matter how cruelly or bizarrely they might manifest, were only twisted versions of the act of love.

*

"I was raised in South Florida," Marcos said once Mona had finished. He didn't offer any sympathy for her or ask follow up questions, which, oddly enough, Mona appreciated. "West Palm Beach. There's a neighborhood called Parker Ridge, where all the Cubans live. It's also where the local branch of Alpha 66 is at. Any idea what that is?"

"Devil-worshipping fraternity of freemasons," Mona guessed.

"Close. It's an anti-Castro terrorist group. My father was a member. He was one of the first wave of Cuban emigrés to the US—came over here when he was a kid, soon after the revolution. *His* father, my grandpa, had been a tobacco importer, in bed with the mob, just like anyone else was if they were doing business in Cuba back then."

Mona could just about see the sinews in Marcos's face muscles tense up as he began to tell the story. He paused to take a long swig from his flask.

"Papa, like most Cubans in America, was a vicious despiser of all things even vaguely left-wing, to say nothing of Castro. So my adolescent rebellious phase, naturally, was sort of hippie punk, and one day I came home with a Che pin on my backpack, even though I barely knew who he was. Papa clocked me so hard he knocked a tooth out."

Marcos opened his mouth into a wide, slightly deranged grin and pointed to his left incisor.

"Porcelain," he said, "but apart from that I didn't see so much of him. That's because, as my mom told me, he did 'volunteer work' after hours. Which is to say he and the rest of the boys at Alpha 66 were plotting a way to take down Castro. This meant he was constantly in danger, and so were we. My parents had fights about it all the time, but nothing ever changed. We stayed in the same house, and Papa stayed out all evening. All the while Ma was the staunchest conservative, you know, had the Reagan/Bush signs standing tall on our little lawn, cursed the hippies well into the mid-eighties.

"The more time he spent away, the more paranoid Ma got. She thought the news was trying to brainwash us. She thought my teachers were trying to brainwash me. She even thought the music on the radio was trying to brainwash us. Come to think of it, she probably wasn't all wrong.

"But the point is, one day Papa disappeared entirely. No goodbye, no letter, no nothing. I came home every single day from school to see Ma crying at the kitchen table. 'He'll be back,' I said, but I doubted it. Then the pictures started showing up in the mail: Papa walking down the streets of Miami with a young blonde. Then a picture of him with a brunette. Eventually, wouldn't you know it, a redhead showed up too. The pictures were from years ago. Someone had been tracking my father and his affairs for a long time. Finally Ma had enough, and she went to one of Papa's Alpha 66 buddies. There had been an explosion that year outside a restaurant in Havana where Fidel's chief of staff was eating—and she knew enough about it to cause problems. So the boys at Alpha 66 eventually gave in and told her that Papa had been assigned to a witness protection program, and he was somewhere unknown out in the Midwest.

"As you can imagine, she didn't get much easier to live with after that. But somehow she did get even more passionate about her anti-Castroism. She blamed Cuba not only for the world's political ills, but for Papa's infidelity too. I suppose it was easier than looking at things as they were and building a new worldview from the ground up.

"Then one night I was raiding the kitchen while Ma was watching the ten o'clock news. And what do you know but Papa's face suddenly appeared on the screen. My back was to the TV, and I can't describe how, but somehow even before the anchor read out the story I just knew to turn around. The graphic said 'Cuban Spy Arrested.' SWAT team had stormed the little condo he was staying in in Kalamazoo. They interviewed the nineteen-year-old girl he was living with: she said he had told her he was an insurance salesman. Pa was being transferred to federal court in DC for the trial.

"You see, it turned out he had been a double agent—he had been relaying Alpha 66's activities back to Castro and company for going on thirty years. While the story was running, Ma just stared blankly at the screen. I didn't dare say anything. I wouldn't have known what to say. Her entire world—every fiber of her angry little being—was based on a lie. I remember the shiver that went down my spine as I realized all of that, in one blinding instant, as I was watching the television flash and flicker, now on to sports, now on to the weather, with the green clouds swirling up the coast. I said to Ma, 'maybe we should watch something else.' She didn't respond, just sat frozen in front of the TV.

"I suppose it should count against me that I left the house for the next few days. But I'd been staying with girlfriends or buddies most of the time those days anyway. And, being a kid, and an angry one, I didn't have much of an idea of how to nurse a broken heart back to health. So I came back to the house at dusk a few days later. And I'll always remember the lizards. A swarm of them—arranged in what looked like a circle on the screen door. They were perfectly still—so still I almost didn't notice them until I reached my hand to turn the handle and got a fistful of reptile instead. It was beautiful actually, the pattern of swirling pale green they made over the netting in the dusk light. Beautiful and terrible. And when I came inside and saw Ma hanging from the ceiling, her face was almost the same shade of green. She must have been dead twenty-four hours. Rope tied to the chandelier light's ceiling fixture. No one had noticed. I guess it would have been another day before the smell would have gotten bad enough. The television was still on. The weather report. And just like before, these green clouds crawled slowly up the coast.

"I stood there for a moment, watching the light from the television dance across her lifeless face. I sat down on the couch and I stared at her corpse like it was the most natural thing in the world. I didn't cry or scream: the shock of what I was looking at was too great for that. But then as I was sitting there staring, my mind completely blank from the sheer horror of it, I was flooded by the most inexpressible feeling. It was as though I was filled by kind of dark, damp fire. I looked at her body, I looked at the rope, I looked at the television. None of it was real to me. The fire radiating through me made that much clear to me. It was as though the world was made out of cardboard and I'd just ripped through it. A terrible, terrible elation. I can't describe it any better than that. But for the first time in my life I knew truly what life and death were, and what freedom was.

"It only lasted a minute. Two at most. Then I snapped out of it and called 911, and a couple of paramedics cut her down. They gave me over to a couple of social workers for the night, but I wouldn't say shit to them. I never stepped foot in that house again—my uncle took me in until I finished up high school in Orlando. And any time anyone asked me if I wanted to talk about it, I gave them such a stare they probably thought I was going to kill them right where they stood."

"You had a paradoxical reaction," Mona said, "like how some people faint or go unconscious when they're overstimulated. You were in a kind of trance."

Marcos shook his head.

"We're in a trance most of our lives," Marcos said, "when we're going about our day, eating, working, fucking. Well, maybe not when we're fucking, with any luck. But for those few moments in that apartment in West Palm I was awake."

By the time he had finished his speech, Mona felt ill, and a thought at the edge of consciousness briefly vexed her: that Marcos's story had been uncomfortably similar to her own. She reached for Marcos's flask, but he turned it on its head and shook it to show it was empty.

"It's getting late. Didn't you say you had a friend to meet?"

Mona checked the time. It was indeed time for her to see Natalie.

"You're going to be all right over here?"

"Oh don't worry about little old me," Marcos said. "Here's my number in case you ever want to rendezvous."

As she walked over toward the train, Mona hoped against hope that she would see Marcos stir in some way from his seat at the bench—that he would get up and walk over to a bar, or pace back and forth along the rim of the park, or even just itch his leg. But for as long as she was able to keep him in her line of vision, he remained still, sitting perfectly straight, with his hands on his knees, faintly illuminated by the lamplight overhead.

*

Natalie twirled her straw around the water in her glass but didn't sip any of it. They had met up in a diner in Chelsea and found a booth in the back corner.

"I need to tell you something," Natalie said.

"Pretty sure," Mona said, "I need to tell you something more. Someone made a threat against my life last night."

"I'm sorry."

"That's your response?"

"No, it's only... Go ahead, I'm listening."

Mona explained about the QR code and the menacing poem. As she did so, it became clear that something terrible had happened to Natalie, too. No obvious sign gave Natalie up, no tears or trembling lips or cuts or bruises. But the subtle intensity of her eyes and the pallor of her face combined to give an ominous effect. Even her short blonde hair seemed to have grown wilder, frizzier, as if Natalie had just recovered from an electric shock.

The hour was late enough that the twilight creatures who are naturally attracted to city diners at odd hours had already set up shop. Two booths over, a man whose stringy gray comb-over covered only a third of his scalp muttered to himself that he *always* had oatcakes at this hour. At the bar, a sullen-faced woman in a cheetah-print dress downed glass after glass of prosecco, each time asking for "just a bit more." A man at the window with dreadlocks and a tie-dye sweatshirt ordered, with the intensity of a general sending his troops into battle, "Hot cakes. Side of bacon. Home fries, *not* French fries and not burnt. Wheat toast and don't stiff me on the jelly."

"The little poem they left you," Natalie said, "you should do what they say. These people are dangerous."

"What people?"

"They're not interested in right or wrong. They're interested in getting what they want."

"Natalie," Mona said, "*what* are you talking about?"

Natalie tapped the table nervously and looked down at her lap.

"It feels almost biblical, you know, how awful things can turn out. When I was over at CRISPR-X it never bothered me—editing genes, changing what it is to be a human, that sort of thing—but now that I look back, it's all so unnatural. No wonder things went the way they did."

"Surely," Mona said impatiently, "you've had the 'am I playing God' conversation with yourself before today."

Natalia gave a crooked smile. "It's not that I worry I'm playing God," she said, "it's more I worry that he's playing me . . . . I don't imagine you know much about the genomics industry over the past decade?"

"This is what you had to tell me?" Mona said.

Their waiter arrived, and they both stared at him in dumb silence for a few moments before ordering a cup of coffee each.

"I'm getting there. But you need a little background to understand. Ten years ago when I started at CRISPR-X, people were convinced, I mean really *convinced* that they were creating the God pill for preventing diseases. *Hundreds* of billions of dollars got poured into these companies that were racing to get there first. People were comparing it with splitting the atom."

"And the fools and their money were soon parted?" Mona asked.

"Very much so. And it was *not* an amicable breakup. Now I don't want to say that mapping the human genome was *useless*. It certainly was not. Diseases can be prevented or mitigated based on the research we did. But by and large, it was a flop; and the people who thought they were going to profit off it all will be the first to tell you that. It turned out that DNA isn't the only thing that matters when it comes to being a human. It's just that it was the only thing we were looking at. We've got this idea that we can solve every problem through the scientific process. But there's something—an entity, a force, whatever you want to call it—that's beyond all that, and it's laughing at us. Laughing at *me*, anyway."

"And what's so funny about you?" Mona asked.

"I was never even that *interested* in genetics," Natalia said. "Hell, I *slept* through biology. But all my life I heard everyone telling me, *biomedical, biomedical, it's the future, Natashenka*. It was like plastics in the sixties. Well, I've put every fiber of my being into it, and from all my work at CRISPR-X I ended up broke."

"*Broke* broke?" Mona asked.

"*Broke* broke," Natalia said, "CRISPR-X was a bust. The fundamental technology was sound, but the way we were going about it was all wrong. Proserpina gave us our shot when it acquired us, and we swung and missed. I didn't even have enough money to pay rent or take care of my cat. Or I didn't until I switched jobs and started doing their dirty work for them."

"Ah, so that's what Head of People really means, eh? But what exactly does dirty work entail?"

"Well," Natalie said, "I was paid a bonus of $50,000 to befriend you, keep track of what you're up to, and get as much information as possible about your interest in Avram Parr's death."

Mona dropped her coffee spoon to the floor and did not pick it up.

"You *what*?"

"But I couldn't keep going on with it. I'm too afraid. I dreamed about you last night. I dreamed it was dark, and a shooting star passed over you and lit up your face. There was blood all around on the grass where you were, and a voice off in the distance screamed and screamed."

"Who were you taking orders from? Jen and Jon?"

"Yes. Jen Rostow is her full name. Jon is just her assistant."

"Am I in serious danger?"

"Of course you are."

"What was supposed to happen next" she asked, "after you had given over whatever information you had on me?"

"They didn't tell me. Jen paid me half on agreement, and the other half is supposed to come forty-eight hours from now. I suppose the idea is they'll have things with you all settled by then."

"Settled," Mona repeated, "In forty-eight hours things with me will be all *settled*."

"I'm so sorry, Mona," Natalia said.

"I imagine then," Mona said sharply, "that that whole 'man with the extra long finger' story was just a tall tale to lure me in."

"No, that was real. I hadn't planned on telling you about it, but once we started talking, I couldn't help but open up. I thought maybe hearing about that could do you good in some way."

"A hell of a lot of good."

Mona continued to glare at Natalia, but eventually let her features soften, and she gave a sigh.

"And where does this leave you?" she asked.

"Well, if they find out what I've done, I'm sure I'm in as much danger as you are. But I can help you now. I can let you know what they're up to."

"And what's to prevent me thinking that you're part of *they*?"

"I guess you've got no reason to," Natalia said. "I really don't know what to say. Other than this. There was something about you that made me feel the need to tell you the truth. Some aura around you. I hope you'll believe that."

"Save it," Mona said. She threw a twenty down on the table and prepared to leave. "One last thing. Any idea who it is Jen reports to now? The man behind the mirror, if you know what I mean?"

"Well, it used to be directly to Parr. Other than that I've just heard a name thrown around. The guy isn't on Proserpina's books, or else I would have met him, but he seems to have a hand in everything. Jen is always excusing herself to go talk things over with him on the phone. The name is Marcos. First name is Ronald? Rollo? Something similar. Is that any help?"

Hildegard 2.0's Dramatic Idyl: Conspiratorial Love

And what about Tower 7, babe,
How did it fall?
I've heard it was from the inside, babe,
I've heard it all.

I've heard about the chimeras, darling,
Half-man half-beast.
The Chinese are breeding these monsters, darling,
To lay us to waste.

Some say the world's getting warmer, honey,
But that's just a fad.
I think their only desire, honey,
is to make us feel bad.

I think they make up these stories, girl,
like a cat paws a mouse.
They just find it awfully amusing, girl,
to enter our house

With their news that's not worth what it's printed on, sweety,
With their 6 o'clock lies
Telling us whom to make idols of, sweety,
And whom to despise.

The truth never was all that simple, doll,
There've always been holes.
What were we told about MK-Ultra, doll,
What were we told?

Everyone has their agenda, snookums,
everyone has their scheme.
Sometimes I think it's a nightmare, snookums,
Life's not a *nice* dream.

Awake! let us walk, you and I, love,
through the smoke and the mist.
If I know but one thing then I know, love:
at least *we* exist.

(10)

Outside the diner, under the bright lights of 8th Avenue, Mona could observe herself shaking, yet she felt strangely cool and rational. She pulled her phone out and texted Marcos.

"You up at this hour?" she asked.

"I'm a spook, Mona," he responded immediately. "Spooks don't sleep."

She got his address and told him she'd be there in fifteen. In the cab over she took deep, slow breaths and ran her finger back and forth along the blade of the knife Del had lent her. Marcos's place was on the thirty-second floor of a glass tower overlooking Columbus Circle. The living room furniture consisted of a tasteful leather couch, a sparsely populated bookshelf, and a Smart TV. The kitchen betrayed no sign of ever having been used.

"What do you eat?" Mona said.

"Takeout."

Marcos opened up the fridge to reveal tonic water, a row of Muscle Milk bottles and some decorative-looking limes. But the limes turned out to be real, and he sliced them up for gin and tonics.

"I take it you don't entertain much," Mona said.

"You don't find me entertaining?"

Out on the balcony the air was cool and the wind whipped their faces. Mona looked down over the balustrade to watch the little cars go round and round the rotary at Columbus Circle. It appeared from the distance that always the same cars went endlessly around. Every so often a horn would sound out softly, plaintively, as though it were only an echo or the remnant of a dream.

"Ever think about what it would be like to fall from here?" Mona said.

"All the time," Marcos said, "I imagine my life flashing before my eyes. People who have near-death experiences report that it really does work that way. They re-live the entire story arc of their lives in that brief moment, like time has stopped. Decades going by in a few seconds."

"Until bang," Mona said.

"Yes," Marcos said, "until bang."

*

Marcos led Mona to the bedroom. As he began to undress her, Mona watched the moving image of the two of them, as though she were a third-party observer, on Marcos's wide mirror-paneled closet doors.

"Wait," Mona said, "do you have handcuffs, or something like that?"

Marcos smiled and went to the closet. As he pulled the door open, Mona saw her reflection slide out of view.

Marcos emerged with a gleaming metal pair. "Police grade," he said.

He stuck them in his pocket and put one arm around Mona's back and one below her thighs, beginning to lift her onto the bed.

"Not for me," she said, "for you."

Marcos took his arm out from under her and gave a quizzical look. Mona smiled as mischievously as she could. For a moment they merely stood in silence, facing off, half-dressed, in this pristine room far above the city. Then Marcos removed his shirt and pants and splayed himself out face up on the bed.

"The keys are on the bedstand," he said.

Mona fastened each of his wrists to a bedpost. "Can you get free at all?" she asked.

In response Marcos only wriggled. Mona watched the soft skin of his wrists press taut against their steel enclosures, as he twisted back and forth, presenting either oblique muscle. He appeared to be fully subdued.

Mona took out her knife from her pocket and released the jagged blade from its hold. She leant over the side of the bed and held it above Marcos's face so that he could see it.

"Now tell me," she said, "why you were following me outside the WeWork station this morning, why you were trailing me at the Proserpina offices, and why you paid Natalie Kulak to keep tabs on me. And no bullshit. I may not be a criminal like you, but I'm desperate enough that I just might take an ear off if you feed me any more lies."

After a moment of shock—his eyes widening and nose emitting a quick brutish snort— Marcos composed himself and grinned widely.

"This," he said, "I do like. A moment of real extremity."

"No philosophizing from you," Mona said, "just explaining. Why have you been following me?"

"It's true," Marcos said, "I suppose I've been less than honest with you. But I can assure you my intentions are benign. I'll gladly lay it all out for you. But you might do me a favor and quit dangling that thing over my face. We wouldn't want your hand to slip."

Mona brought the knife to her side. "Talk," she said.

Marcos untensed his body to tell his tale, but not before giving a last wriggle of the wrists, as though testing whether he might be able to snake his way out of the cuffs through some previously untried contortion.

"The fact is that things are a little more dire than I've let on. But I didn't know yet if I could trust you with the truth. Parr was in fact killed by agents of the state, with collaboration from New York's finest. Whether your police friend Aldo actively participated, or whether he's just covering for someone higher up, is a matter for conjecture.

"About five years ago the Feds tapped Parr to do some work for them under the table. They knew that he was operating at the cutting edge of bioengineering, and they knew he had business in China, where the restrictions on experiments are a little looser. Particularly, the Bureau was interested in what are being called 'chimeras'—half-human, half-animal hybrids that Chinese scientists have developed, if *developed* is really the word—in which they can grow kidneys and other organs that they'll use for research or sell. It's a rather clever scheme. Humans have rights. Animals have rights. But these half-human half-animal chimeras... well, it's a bit of a gray area.

"Parr was recruited to dig up any compromising information he could about these Chinese CEOs and to pass it on to his handlers. He proved, however, to be rather *too* good at his task. I suppose Parr's handlers had figured that Parr would be tempted, and so he himself would become properly blackmailable, and thus controllable. But it didn't happen that way. Parr kept his hands clean. But now he had a pretty fair amount of unsavory intelligence on Chinese *and* American power players. He knew he was sitting pretty—he could play the two nations off one another to get access to the latest and most controversial medical advances. Unfortunately, the Feds know just what to do with ambitious young people who go rogue. Parr was not quite enough of a public figure for anyone to care if his supposed cause of death was bullshit. So they got a couple of agents to break into his place, tie him down, and inject him with enough fentanyl to kill a small horse. Since that happened, I've been working my ass off to gather proof, and I've also been rather concerned with not getting bumped off myself. So when I discovered someone had been talking to the cops about Parr and asking questions at WeWork, I figured I'd have her tailed. Sorry to hurt your feelings, but it's simply the tricks of the trade. And now if you'll kindly release me...."

Mona continued to stand over him and ran her finger along the blade's edge to assure herself of its sharpness. But the test was too thorough, and she pricked herself. She put her finger in her mouth and tongued the droplet of salty blood.

"Surely," she said, "you can prove all this to me without my letting you out just yet. I wouldn't want to set you loose before I know whether you're friend or foe."

Marcos grimaced.

"My phone is in the left pocket of my pants," he said, "password is 4321."

"Clever one," Mona said. She slid the phone out and unlocked it.

"Search my email for a message from your friend Aldo," Marcos said.

Mona found a message from gennaro.aldo@nypd.org, dated February 28, 2016, which read as follows:

> To Mr. Roland Marcos or Associate at Osiris Integrative,
> This is Detective Jerry Aldo at the NYPD. I have tried to reach you at your purported work address several times. I have also rung your purported office telephone several times. This is my last try. Although I do not yet have warrant to search your property or charge you with any crime, I must warn you that my fellow lawmen and I can make life extraordinarily difficult for you. Consider this a personal warning. You must cease shielding Avram Parr at once. He will have to return to New York eventually. And when he does so we will deal with him swiftly and most severely. I advise that you excuse yourself from this situation before it's too late.
>
> With regards,
> Detective Jerry Aldo

Just when Mona had finished reading this email, a text message notification appeared onscreen. It was from someone named "Chrissie Rose." The message said, *let's do it tonight.*

"Your friend Chrissie Rose just wrote you," Mona said. She watched Marcos closely but no change in expression appeared on his face. "Should I tell her you're a little... indisposed?"

"What did she say?"

"She said 'let's do it tonight.' Sounds like a real lady. What do you think I should tell her?"

"You can tell her whatever you please," Marcos said, "seeing as you've got me tied to the bedposts. But I'm more interested in what you thought of Aldo's email."

"Let's just say I found it very piquant," Mona said. "I don't quite know what it's proof of, however."

"It's proof," Marcos said, "that Aldo was harassing me and trying to get to Parr. You're looking for answers about who had it in for Parr. I'm telling you. I can't do any better than that, Mona."

Mona looked his sinewy body up and down.

"If I had wanted to hurt you," Marcos said, "I would have done so weeks ago."

This particular detail seemed undeniable. Everything about Marcos gave the impression of one who would not dally about, if he meant to inflict pain. Mona knew she now had two choices. She could either leave him to rot here on his huge bed, high above city's glittering expanse, or she could take her chances with Marcos as an ally—or, if not an ally, then someone who might lead her toward where she needed to go. Mona put her hand down on the bedstand and picked up the key.

She felt suddenly as though a force beyond her control were entering into the logic of the evening. She felt her skin shiver as she took in simultaneously the bright emptiness of the room, the cool metal of the key in her hand, Marcos's lithe body, and the lights of the toy-sized city down below, burning outside through the cold night.

"And if I let you free now," Mona said, "you're not going to strangle me right here in your room or anything drastic like that."

"Nothing drastic like that," Marcos said. "At worst I might give you a love tap."

"Where?" Mona said.

She put the key into the hole and released Marcos from his bind. She kept her other hand clenched around the knife.

Marcos merely sat up and looked into her eyes. Mona got the sense he was looking for something there—a sign that might reveal to him how best to proceed.

"Don't you want to respond to your friend Chrissie?" Mona said.

"You respond. Tell her that I'm with someone more interesting right now and my business with her will have to wait until tomorrow evening."

"And what is your *business* with her?"

"We're going over my tax returns," Marcos said. "Chrissie is my accountant. A good one too. Very thorough."

Mona laughed. "And here I was thinking up until this point that you were a good liar."

"I *am* a good liar," Marcos said, "always have been."

He rose from the bed and stood in front of Mona, close enough that she could feel her skin grazed by his breath. She watched his broad chest rise and fall.

"Well don't boast about it," she said brightly, "it's extremely gauche. Honestly, I wonder how much of what you've told me tonight has any truth to it at all."

"There are things that are true," Marcos said, his face so close now that he needed only to whisper, "that don't necessarily line up with logic. Sometimes the truth is personal, it's something you feel."

Mona touched her hand to his face, ran her hand along its contours before extending her fingers around his throat, squeezing softly at first and then with more and more force. Marcos made no reaction, only staring into her eyes, until she finally loosened her grip and guided his face in toward her own. Later that evening she would bite his lip so hard she broke the skin—and asked him if he could feel the truth of *that*.

From the Diary of Avram Parr

September 21, 2015

"The present offers no way out. That is not the least of its virtues."

I read this the other day in a recently published anarchist pamphlet. (I like to keep myself abreast of the anarchists: at least they know that all society boils down to relations of power.) Their proposition is one with which those far enough on either side of the so-called political spectrum can agree. But the majority, clustering toward the middle, despise this truth. Within the morass of the present, like prey animals immured in swampland, they struggle to escape. And the more they struggle the deeper they sink.

Some people seek escape from the present through television or their phones: they are in effect hooked up to a hypnosis machine, in between eight-hour-per-day shifts of sustenance labor for the benefit of the system by which they're hypnotized; and then they die.

Some people seek escape through illegal drugs. They die quickly, or else they are kept on life support by psychiatric institutions and barely legal pharmaceuticals that convert their hatred of the system into profit.

Some seek escape through collective action. Up until a few hundred years ago, this was a viable method. If, for instance, one was displeased with the King, one could form a corporate entity of dissenters and found a new land. But today there is no more new land. There are few Kings either, but that fact is misleading. A King or a Queen, when it comes down to it, is merely the person whose power goes beyond the law. Today the crowd is the King. Whichever way the crowd moves, the law moves. Ergo, the crowd is king.

Another way to think of the King of today is to think of him as the community of storytellers: Whoever has the best story has the order behind the law. (Just look at how the laws, of the United States have changed over the last few centuries based on the stories its inhabitants tell themselves.) And yet we are not conscious of telling ourselves these stories, and for the most part we do not exactly know where the stories come from. Most storytellers have been hypnotized into telling stories that have been programmed into them, just as one might program a computer.

Thus I do not look to the present for a way out. I look to the distant future: to a set of possibilities about which 99.9 percent don't dare dream. And I work to plant the seed for this future in my own lifetime.

What are the possibilities of the distant future? A breakaway civilization: that is the ideal. But I'm still missing the elements that might allow it to function. I am currently limited by land, by law, but more than anything, by public opinion.

The problem of land itself is solved easily enough: by sea-steading or by the colonization of Mars. The problem of law is solved easily enough if the climate is right; law is, at the final analysis, only a codification of whichever way the wind blows.

The problem of law is only a subset of the problem of public opinion. Change opinion, and you have, in effect, changed the law.

October 2, 2015

An odd conversation with Mona Veigh, of Hildegard. I do not usually find myself wrong-footed by my business associates. But now that it has happened, I must say I'm more intrigued than miffed. I do not yet understand her motivations, and when I do not understand a person's motivations it is difficult to know how to enter into a symbiotic relation with them. But it occurred to me today that she may be capable of more than what I foresaw. I don't know yet how great of an asset she might be.

"What human problems do you believe Hildegard might someday solve?" I asked. It is one of my standard questions for team leads.

"None," she said, "although hopefully it will create a few new ones." I asked her to explain herself.

"The philosopher Søren Kierkegaard," she said, "discovered his purpose in life when he was a young man. He realized it wasn't to make life easier for anyone—the industrial revolution was taking care of that just fine—it was to make life more difficult. He meant he wanted people to see that there's a whole world beyond what was conventionally thought to be true. Hildegard wants people to see that there's a whole world beyond what we think of as machines."

This was not satisfactory to me and I requested that she re-phrase her answer without unhelpful analogies or rhetorical flourishes.

"Hildegard," she said, "does things that can't quite be accounted for logically. Or, rather, they can be accounted for logically, but it strains the mind to do so. I can point you to dozens of poems that show what I mean. I believe the program's purpose, if it can be said to have a purpose, is to show that all language is a reflection of some preordained ur-language that we can only get the faintest glimpse of. This isn't a radical idea—at least not among poets. Most of them would admit listening to some kind of inner voice along the lines of what I'm describing. But I'm not a poet, and I don't have an inner voice. So I had to invent a machine that would help me eavesdrop."

It seems to me there is a small but a nontrivial chance that her comments are more than obscurantist gibberish; I must investigate further.

(11)

Mona woke up in Marcos's bed the next morning feeling as well rested as she had in months. It was soon after dawn. Light had just begun to filter in through Marcos's long curtains. He lay next to her, above the covers, splayed out on his back. Mona took a moment to notice the angry, determined look his face took on in sleep, before she rose to inspect the apartment.

She began with the bathroom. But all he had in his medicine cabinet was Vyvanse, Dapper Dan Pomade, a toothbrush, toothpaste, and teeth-whitening strips. The kitchen revealed no more than it had the previous night—except this time Mona opened the butter drawer in the fridge and found two dozen packs of grape jelly stacked atop one another with appalling neatness. Mona moved onto the living room, with its scantily filled bookshelf.

In fact, Mona always took an interest in her paramours' bookshelves, and always ended up feeling sad and uneasy by the end of the inspection. Marcos's was comprised of three rows of thick, burnished oak. A few dozen trendy or once-trendy novels from the past decade leant against one another on the top row. The middle section was mostly empty: one book on tax off-shoring, one on hypnotism, and one on color theory. On the bottom were an assortment of would-be coffee table books (for all the apartment's size, Marcos had no actual coffee table) and a few Penguin Classics.

Mona flipped through each of the classics from front to back. Some of them had at least been cracked open. In the Marcus Aurelius she even found underlining, and in Nietzsche's *Human, All Too Human* she found both underlining and a slip of paper. The paper bore a neatly penned list of names:

Blau
Himmel
Gravesend
Bloom
Krasnik
Rosas

Something about the list struck her and Mona tucked it into her back pocket. Then she read the underlined aphorism on the page it had marked: "Opinions and Fish.—We are possessors of our opinions as of fish—that is, in so far as we are possessors of a fish pond. We must go fishing and have luck—then we have *our* fish, *our* opinions. I speak here of live opinions, of live fish. Others are content to possess a cabinet of fossils—and, in their head, 'convictions.'"

Mona frowned. This aphorism had been born out of a desperate, lonely genius's struggle against centuries of received wisdom. It annoyed her to imagine Marcos underlining it after a glance and equating it with his own opportunistic nihilism.

And yet she didn't know why she was being so hard on this man whose body she had just enjoyed. At a certain point last night Mona had begun to feel refreshed by his cold shallowness, his smiling unconcern with all she held dear. Whether or not he was well-read, he was clever and successful. No grand understanding of the poetic tradition was required for where he meant to take his life. He did not need great literature, and great literature did not need him.

Everyone was doing just fine, thank you. Except for me, Mona thought, me and my Emily Dickinson shut-in life. She cursed the intelligence and intransigence that made her an anachronism. She slammed the book shut.

"Getting some early morning reading in?" Marcos said.

He had crept behind her and now stood in his boxer shorts, stretching out his sinewy body. Mona checked her pocket to make sure the slip of paper was safely interred, and then put the book back on the shelf.

"Early bird gets the wisdom," she said drearily.

"I was thinking we could get brunch at the place around the corner. You'll love their eggs Nicoise."

"There's actually some reading I want to get done today," Mona said. "I have to head out in a minute."

"Your iambic pentameter makes a better lover than I do."

"Something like that."

Marcos shook his head faux-ruefully.

"I wonder what it is exactly that's wrong with you."

"This, I take it, is your idea of pillow talk."

"I don't mean it in a cruel way," Marcos said, and yet his smile widened unpleasantly, as though he had just scratched an especially irksome itch. "I just mean there has to be something a *bit* wrong with someone so dedicated to something so useless."

A familiar nausea coursed through Mona's stomach.

"Is this truly the conversation you want to be having right now, as you stand before me in your little shorts?"

"I don't see why not. I *know* what's wrong with me, after all. I've studied it and made peace with it. But I'm trying to get to the bottom of *you*. See, I know from discussions with Jen that Proserpina is still flush with cash, and I know from just one night with you that you would still be successful in that world if you wanted to be. But what I don't know is how poetry has you so in thrall that you abandoned the rest of existence."

Something about his out-of-place earnestness got through to Mona. She realized that she had never quite asked herself this question directly, and that at the moment she was dangerously near an answer.

"Do you even look at that elegant code you created? Does it still even exist?"

"What does it matter? The only person who really had a handle on what I was doing and took a real interest in it was Parr, and he's dead."

"So you burn it to the ground to spite the cruel world."

"It's not the sort of thing you can burn. But the repo where it's hosted is pretty difficult to find, if that's what you're asking."

"And all this so you can work on some long poem about how the sky is blue." Mona gave him a shocked look.

"Excuse me?"

"Jen told me you were writing something like that."

"Oh for God's sake," Mona said, "I'm really not."

"How's this," Marcos said, "tell me what so entrances you about poetry, and I'll tell you something I didn't tell you before about Parr. Think about it while I order up coffee and breakfast. I don't need you to answer in rhyme or anything. Just tell me the truth. What's really behind Mona Veigh?"

⁂

That there was a reality deeper than what was commonly called reality: this was the idea that had guided Mona in her youth. Yet she had felt no desire to share this notion with anyone. It was fine to keep it private, to dive down into the well of the numinous whenever she needed refreshment, and dry herself off thoroughly before coming back in contact with the world. The world and the word—these were two separate realms for her. The former was the drab dominant force of life, while the latter, though its magic could only break through from time to time, covered the world with its splendor whenever it did emerge, and made mundane life worth getting through.

And into the glow of the word sometimes even the world could be accommodated. When Mona was blessed by a poem—when its rhythm informed her gait and tingled her spine—then it would shiver across all that was external to her, too. Its rhythm would be in the lamplight diffused along grainy gravel on an autumn evening stroll from her apartment toward the city. It would be in the faint whir of a plane far overhead, sailing like a leaf in the wind toward LaGuardia. It was in the smell of empanadas along Northern Boulevard, in the reflective puddles dotting depressed areas of the sidewalk on rainy days, in the cold west wind.

The rhythm would even find its way into the ambience of the sad little Chinese restaurant on 37th Avenue where Mona would go to refuel, into the gently chiming music on the stereo and into the dirty, fluorescently lit bathroom. In fact Mona found that the more abject a place was, the more receptive it was, somehow, to being filled by the soft light of poetic trance. Poetic trance liked the lowly or degraded: the lowly or degraded was at least honest. This in contrast to all that was puffed up and shiny, which tried to imitate the world of wonders Mona felt she knew so well, and to bring it into realms where it did not belong. The poetic trance could not abide dinner parties where expensive food was treated as an end in itself and not simply sustenance, or high-strung political arguments, or upscale cocktail lounges with mood lighting, or advertisements for soft mohair beanies and luxury leather gloves.

Not that she minded soft mohair beanies and luxury leather gloves per se. Actually, Mona *could* take pleasure in good clothes, silly soap operas, and the radio's vulgar earworms. What she minded was any attempt on the part of these ephemera to claim real importance. For Mona it was clear what was ultimate, and when sham art or wordy morality tried to pass itself off as of ultimate importance, this not only offended her sensibility but hit her in the gut with a sense of impending doom—for she knew that in the battle between the world and the word the victor was not guaranteed.

She could not say how exactly it had come to be that these two realms got so starkly separated in her mind. Sure, there were pat psychological explanations involving phrases like trauma reaction, defense mechanism, fantasy, and compensation. She could still taste her childhood loneliness, the gloomy, slowly lurching elevator she'd take up to her mother's apartment, as her stomach dropped. And she could still feel a warm wave come over her body when she thought of the public library on 82nd Street, where the tiny plastic chairs were too small even for her small young body—but she did not mind the ache in her back as she twisted this way and that across the seat, thumbing through mystery stories and atlases and zoological catalogs, and, of course, poems.

Poems: those portals into realms of pure word. The first one she could recall transporting her was Edna St. Vincent Millay's sonnet beginning "What lips my lips have kissed and where and why." Mona had not even had her first kiss when she read it. But that was not important.

What was important were the three words at the beginning of the next line: "I have forgotten." This business of forgetting stirred her, even at the age of twelve. It was precocious nostalgia, an inkling of desuetude to come. The poem's subject, of a time and a place when memories are gone and what has come to pass is meaningless, blended so paradoxically well with the poem's easy, almost sing-songy prosodic structure, which Mona would soon learn to identify as iambic pentameter, that stalwart of English poetry. She would learn, too, the hypothesis that this national rhythm of England and later of the whole Anglophone world had sprung from Bronze Age Greek totemic rites, in which the ring-around-the-rosy dance steps imitated the hobbling gait of partridges in mating season.

But for now all she knew was that the rhythm and the words of the poem were as one. The combination spoke to a part of her she could not describe but had felt within herself since she was old enough to be conscious of feeling anything at all. She'd later read the words of a clever poet who described the magic of poetry as existing *between* the words of a given poem; this space between the words was like a series of fissures in the composition of the world itself. And although at the time Mona would not quite have been able to phrase it that way, she could still feel herself falling through.

And from then on it was a trapdoor she might fall down at any moment. The feeling could visit her anywhere. It was odd and it could be frightening. But mostly it was sublime—especially when she was very young. In those years, up through early adolescence, it felt perfectly natural to keep this magnificent secret: the whole world of childhood was a magnificent secret, and poetry was simply the aspect of it that was most intense. Her middle school teacher didn't quite know what to make of it when she took a volume of Robert Browning with her to the basketball court at recess, but there were so many other children that required more immediate attention. So no one bothered her those mild afternoons, and to this day she still associated a bouncing basketball's rhythmic clatter with the tripping cadences of Browning's *Dramatic Idyls*, and the chain-link cages that boxed in basketball courts all over the country still felt to her palms, when she ran her hands along the metal, like a gateway to freedom.

Adolescence made poetry, and everything else, more difficult. But it gave her plenty of license to be moody. Oddly enough Mona did not give vent to her moods by writing poetry herself. She hardly saw the point. What she sought in the realm of the word was an ineluctable, divine sensation—not a mode of self-expression. It was enough for Mona that others had gone into the depths and brought something back. She felt no imperative to mix halcyon meter, rhyme, and timbre with mundane lived experience. Plus there was the fact that nothing much happened to her to write poetry about. She did not fall in love. She did not go to battle. She did not have a queen to glorify or the sort of faith that might induce her to justify the ways of God to man. She had her room in her mother's apartment on 79th Street, well lit and reasonably quiet most of the time, and she had the train ride to high school and back, and friends who were just as smart and sarcastic as she but who still did not have access to her secret world.

She had one teacher in high school who actually taught poetry well. He would say very little about the poems themselves. But he advised his students to read each poem he assigned three times, away from screens, and preferably under a tree—if the weather was reasonable and there happened to be one nearby. He shared with them the words of a scholar (Mona could not for the life of her track down its source, and now suspected that he may have made it up himself), that a poem was a real poem if you could insert the word *not* before its crucial line without doing the poem any injury. The teacher's name was Mr. Adler. He was a puffy-faced, balding man with small, delicate hands. He gave Mona her first edition *Norton Anthology of English Literature* as a gift when the class ended, and looked down at his feet and seemed to stifle a tremor when he shook her hand goodbye.

After that, as far as Mona was concerned, her formal education in poetry and in literature in general had ended. She disliked her later teachers, who talked of themes and taught to the test. Either a person knew what poetry was, Mona believed, or they did not. And no amount of erudition or enthusiasm or fashionable opinions could make up for it if one did not. The knowing was not intelligence, but the ability to hear the sound of something incommunicable. It was an ability one could nurture not by an accumulation of anything but by the sloughing off of whatever stood between a person and the terrible realms of delight Mona had noticed so starkly that first night with the Millay poem.

So the rest of Mona's poetic education was to her now, as she looked back on it, not a compendium of what she had learned but a series of scenes, each of which illuminated a particular shade of poetic sensibility. Here she was bicycling over the Queensboro Bridge, at midnight in hot, languid summer. She was off to a party, to see friends, or to see a boy: it didn't matter much which. What mattered was the rhythm of her legs pumping against the pedals, and the lights of the city before her, sharpening over time from the indistinct bright fat blur of the journey's beginning into crisp emblems of all future happiness and love. Here—here was poetry, she thought, and she knew that certain meters or phrases would recall this sensation later on, though the sense of the words would have nothing to do with cities or lights.

She went to a leafy little college in New England, and walked through wooded paths off campus and recited verse to herself. But these four years, which she felt ought to have been the most conducive to a poetic education in principle, were in practice nearly fatal to it. Mona found that the study of literature had been ground down into mere fodder for charlatans and careerists to munch on. And it was incredible to see how plump they grew, lustily gobbling up actual literature and converting it into polemical, willfully obtuse, or downright nonsensical droppings.

It was then that she started studying computer science in earnest. She was at college: she figured she might as well learn something. It was around that time that neural networks were becoming big. These were the sorts of artificial intelligence systems that could teach *themselves*, instead of merely reaching into a repository of knowledge that had been programmed into them. Mona had heard from her mother about a company called Deep Mind, which built a program that learned chess from scratch, and then became superior to all previous humans and other chess engines, over the course of six or seven hours. The computer science department was filled with the sort of people Mona liked: they didn't talk much.

And if poetry continued to follow her those years, it was more like a shameful secret than a blissful avocation. She knew she couldn't quit it, but she also knew the role it played in her life was becoming every day more gnarled and inward. One day she even injured herself for poetry: It was a Sunday and she decided to take one of her rambles through the woods leading out from campus. She had her eyes fixed on the umber leaves of oaks above her, and the geometric patterns of sky that fit like puzzle pieces between them. She rushed along the path in the dusk, humming dactyls from Lattimore's translation of *The Odyssey*, in order to keep the rhythm up: *dum* da da *dum* da da *dum* da da ... *DUM*. A low-hanging branch interrupted her in the rudest way possible—by cracking her across the face. Her mouth bled all the way back to her dorm, and she could feel her left incisor jiggling. The local dentist, a very rustic fellow, said he'd never heard a story quite like that. Mona did not ask him what other sorts of things he'd never heard of. She wasn't doing fricatives very well. It was a comic reminder but she took it to heart all the same: that only pain would come from her obsession. She thought of an anthropological study she'd read weeks before in class, where once a year a remote tribe in Papua New Guinea organized a big festival of song and dance, and then all those artistic souls, who had touched the crowd with their music and movement, were ceremonially burned with torches—to compensate for the grief they had caused.

*

By the time Marcos had come back with coffee Mona still did not know how she would answer him about her love of poetry. They sat down on his couch and Mona took long, thoughtful sips from her Styrofoam cup, giving Marcos a look as though to indicate that speaking and drinking coffee at the same time was impossible.

"Tell me what you thought of this morning, and then I'll answer you," she said finally.

Marcos took out his phone and pulled up an email from Parr, dated February 29, 2016. It read:

> Roland,
> Effective immediately, please extend your security detail to all WorkLife co-working stations. These offices are under the Proserpina umbrella, and the scope of our operation now includes them. I've appended a list of liaisons who will report to you in the event of any notable activity. I will be on a spiritual retreat in Death Valley April 15–30th (my first real vacation in seven years), but will arrange via Jen Rostow to be reachable in case of emergency.
> AP

"So while he was supposed to be in the desert pitching a tent and finding a Lord Cthulu–shaped hole in his heart during his ayahuasca trip, he was actually in a penthouse being dead," Mona said.

"Exactly," Marcos said.

"It could have just been a scheduling error."

"You knew Parr as well as I did," Marcos said, "and I think we could both agree he's not the sort to make a scheduling error."

"Or it could just be that he ended his vacation early."

"Could be. Or it could be that he was up to something that he didn't want anyone to know about, and used the vacation as a cover. It could be that he and Jen Rostow were the only two people who knew exactly what, and now one of those people is dead."

"Now you're saying that Parr's publicity director, in cahoots with the federal government, lured him to New York and then murdered him. You watch a lot of TV, don't you?"

"All I'm saying is it's a lead worth following. Why don't we drop in on her at the WorkLife station after we've finished breakfast."

"I don't think Jen especially wants to see me again," Mona said.

"But she wouldn't mind seeing me. I'm her trusted agent. You can wait in the wings till I get the scoop. Now quit stalling, don't think that I'm going to forget. You still need to talk to me about poetry."

Mona looked into Marcos's eyes. He wouldn't understand. There were few people who would. Oddly enough, Parr had been one of them, toward the end. Perhaps because he had completely ignored the world of letters in his youth, he was unburdened by fashionable nonsense, and she was able to convey to him at least a piece of what made poetry essential to her. It surprised Mona to find that he became interested, until she realized that he was one of those strange people interested in knowledge for its own sake.

Marcos, on the other hand, was the sort who used knowledge only instrumentally. That much was clear enough from his smile. Probably he had some devious reason for wanting to know the answer to this question, though Mona could not for the life of her imagine what it might be. She walked to the door and slipped on her shoes

"Keeps me off the streets," she said, "now let's move."

(12)

Once Mona and Marcos got downtown, they hit a traffic jam. At 14th Street Mona told the cabbie they could walk from there, and the two of them hopped out into the chilly afternoon. Several blocks down on Greenwich a crowd had formed.

"Looks like all this hubbub is right outside the WorkLife," Marcos said.

"Maybe it's free tapas day in the rec room," Mona said.

But as they got closer Mona saw the police barricade. A tall, muscular cop with a neck tattoo and a small cop with a handlebar mustache both stood with their arms folded.

"What's the situation, officers?" Marcos asked.

"Accident," the tall cop said, "hit and run. Crime scene now."

Past the barricade, an ambulance was parked in the middle of the street. One could just make out the prongs of a gurney poking out from it. All around Mona and Marcos, pedestrians were pacing back and forth and craning their heads to try to get a look at the body.

"Go around!" the small cop shouted, "this is a crime scene here! No one comes through. Go around!"

A teenager in a Supreme T-shirt was bouncing around in front of the barriers, at times taking photos of the policemen, and at times taking selfies.

"Yeah, fools!" he said, "go around."

Mona shot him a look.

"My friend was a witness," he said to her, as though she had asked, "he's talking to the detective right now. . . . He said it was totally batshit! Some dude in an Escalade hopped up onto the sidewalk and nailed this lady, almost like he was *trying* to mow her down. Then he sped off into the sunset, just like that. Didn't even stop to say oopsie daisy."

"Stand back!" the small cop said to the teenager, "you're too close to the barriers. Stand back!"

"It's a public street right here," the teenager said, "I know my rights!"

"Can you use your security badge to get us through?" Mona whispered to Marcos.

"It doesn't work as well with real police."

"You wanna get cuffed and put in the back of a squad car?" the small cop shouted at the teenager.

"Easy now," the tall cop said.

Under cloud cover the afternoon had become prematurely dark. The crosswalk signal at the end of the street was broken, so that at intervals the flashing red hand and the silver blinking body blended together into a single self-contradictory sign. Rain began to fall. The Duane Reade on the corner displayed in its windows three banners that read "How I Look," "How I Feel," and "What I Need Now," in lavender, vermillion, and mauve, respectively.

"What law am I breaking?" the teenager shouted, "what law am I breaking! Why don't you go catch some real criminals? There's nothing you can do to me. My friend's a valuable witness!"

"Just stand back a few feet please," the tall cop said, "until the area is clear."

"Do you think it will be much longer, officer?" Mona asked.

"Ten or fifteen minutes, my guess," the tall cop said.

The teenager, still staring at the two policeman, walked backward ten paces. Then he threw his shoulders back and folded his arms as if to mirror them.

"Not because you told me to," he said, "only because I'm a nonviolent person."

And, as though his capitulation had turned the key, the ambulance's engine revved up and the police at the other end of the street prepared to make way. For whatever reason—perhaps it was the shock of the Village's brownstone tranquility having been interrupted, perhaps because the accident was near to a transit hub for the PATH train to Jersey, or perhaps because it is simply in the nature of New York crowds to get out of hand—the number of gawkers had more than doubled since Mona and Marcos first arrived. Presently they found themselves shoved up against the teenager amid the bustle.

"Have you guys ever seen a dead body before?" he asked.

Mona stared at him as icily as she could manage, and Marcos cleared his throat, but the boy was undeterred.

"My friend said it was fucking *nasty*. Like someone had taken her head and straight up uncorked it. Pop! Just like that. And even though you expect blood to look like ketchup, like in the movies, he said it was way darker and the dying lady's lips went a weird blue color, and her nose twitched."

"Your friend is very observant," Mona said.

"You gotta be, in this city," the teenager said.

The ambulance had gone out the other side of the street, but the crowd had not yet been cleared. Mona and Marcos and the teenager held tight against the bars of the barricade so as not be swept up by the crowd.

"My own personal theory," the teenager continued, "is that if you look closely enough at anything, it turns out that it's not what it seems. Like yin and yang, you know? Like anything that looks totally perfect looks that way because deep down it's bullshit, and anything that looks like a total dumpster fire has probably got a pot of gold inside once the fire cools down. Like a special, nonflammable pot of gold, I guess."

"Our little philosopher," Marcos said.

"Take you, for instance," the teenager said to Mona, "you're dressed kind of schlumpy, and you look depressed or like you've got a gluten intolerance you don't know about or something, and you've been biting your nails. Gross. But maybe that's 'cause you're trying to hide how deep down you think you're all that, but you don't want other people to think you think that, so you overcompensate, or undercompensate, or whatever. You get it."

Mona's irritation blossomed into rage. She bit her lip as the teenager continued.

"And this guy in the suit, what's his deal? I'd watch out for him if I was you. How do you even know him, anyway?"

Mona swiveled her head to give Marcos a once-over, then turned back to the teenager. "I try to watch out for anyone in a suit who's not inside the Goldman Sachs building or some shit like actively defrauding people," he continued, "cause what kind of chaos has he got to be hiding underneath? What's his secret? What's so scary to him that he's got to button it all up? I don't like that smile, either. It's a serial killer's smile."

"Have you known many serial killers?" Marcos asked good-naturedly.

"I've listened to podcasts about them," the teenager replied. "Anyway, I'm just saying—this guy's worth watching out for. He's got a little American Psycho in him, you feel me?"

Suddenly the police officers abandoned their post, and the barriers were removed. The crowd flooded through onto Perry Street, where a dark stain could be found on the curb. Mona felt a hand on the small of her back and assumed it was Marcos's, but when she turned she found that it belonged to a squat, energetic old woman attempting to push her out of the way. Marcos, however, had got lost in the crowd. A few feet away Mona saw a man in a suit and called out to him, but when he turned his head she saw the face of a middle-aged man with a thick gray mustache.

She picked up her pace and elbowed past slow-moving gawkers who meant to get a glimpse of blood. The co-working station was just across the street from where the accident had occurred. The fabric of its awning rippled in the wind. Mona craned her head and glimpsed Jen Rostov standing underneath it. Jen appeared to be taping up some kind of sign to the door. Mona nearly shouted her name, but intuition held her back. It would seem odd to be present at this very moment. And without Marcos, the plan to get information about Parr's pre-death itinerary would have to wait. Mona dallied under cover of a nearby bus stop till Jen had passed. Then she approached the door.

It took Mona several times re-reading it before she could fully apprehend the meaning of the sign Jen had posted. Her first instinct was to forbid its content from entering her mind, as though she could will away what the words meant by an act of concerted ignorance. But this was no use. She re-read the note once more for good measure. It read:

> *The Greenwich Village WorkLife co-working station is closed today in memoriam of Natalie Kulak, who is recently deceased owing to an unfathomably tragic automobile accident. Natalie was a total team player and will be painstakingly missed. In lieu of flowers, please consider a donation to Connected for Good, the charitable disbursements branch of the Proserpina decentralized finance constellation. May Natalie forever rest in power.*
> —Jen Rostov

The only person Mona had talked to about Natalie was Marcos. Mona turned around to face the crowd and make sure that her besuited companion was not watching her from some high perch, and smiling his incomprehensible smile. But Marcos was nowhere to be found.

*

A low hum, then the rickety, irregular clang of the F train lurching forward, as though grudgingly, across worn rails. Now on her way home, Mona felt more acutely than ever before on the subway the fact of its being underground. She needed to think, and to think she needed to breathe. Yet the air seemed to fight her off when she inhaled. Mona attempted to take a slow, deep breath in through the nose and out through the mouth—a breath of the kind that wellness gurus prescribe for times of crisis—but this only made her more aware of the vulnerable, panicky heart pumping inside her.

She decided to fix her eyes on something steadying. The gray tiles through the train window at first appeared to do the trick. But soon the grid of squares began to mock her with its repetitiveness: so much material in existence, neither beautiful nor true, just a sensory input, happening over and over again as the train rushed on forward, like madness. Mona brought her gaze back to the inside of the train. Across her a woman with long, matted hair sat with her head slumped on her lap, appearing to be dead. Behind the woman, an ad for a university boasted that it ranked "13th out of 978 in upward mobility." A crowd of broad-shouldered professionals entered at 42nd Street Bryant Park. At 49th Street, a man with the goiter on his neck the size of a golf ball took mincing steps onto the train car and shook a paper Pepsi cup full of change. Mona cast her glance down.

Mona silently formed the words of the poem she liked to say to herself in times of most acute distress. It was, like so much else in her life, strange and abstract and self-referential, and yet she found that it possessed a talismanic power to bring her comfort.

"Stop all the clocks," she murmured, "turn off the telephone, prevent the dog from barking with a juicy bone."

It was a poem about death and the attendant feelings of desolation. That was what it was about on the outside, at least. But what made the poem resonant for Mona was that the author's actual intent was for the poem to be ridiculous, owing to its jagged, doggerel-esque prosody and banal images. Yet in the ninety or so years since it was written it had morphed into something eerily different.

The poem had originally appeared in a verse play, *The Ascent of F6*, and served as a mock eulogy for the play's villain, transforming death's plangent wail into the drab pomposity of an official statement. With its uncontrolled rhythm and unserious pronouncements ("put crepe bows round the white necks of the public doves, let the traffic policeman wear black cotton gloves," Mona whispered, as the train came to a shrill halt at 5th and 53rd), the poem's main thrust seemed to be that there is a force sweeping over the world, unstoppable in its voracious banality, which will assimilate all that was once heroic or villainous—all that was once terrible, or awe-inspiring, or simply human—into its cunning orbit of nothingness.

But now the standards by which it could have been judged as a parody, and thus by which a complex ironic meaning could be derived from it, had eroded. Few now noticed the poem's prosodic unevenness. And the use of banal rhymes had become so familiar through pop songs that those of "Stop All the Clocks" no longer registered as intentionally bad. So what was once a parody of the tragic had come to seem truly tragic. The poem had even been read in the climactic funeral scene of a Hollywood romantic comedy.

Mona memorized the poem, she supposed, as a reminder that the world she loved so much was ending. Whole layers of meaning and stylistic nicety in literature were being erased by the simple passage of time. And worst of all, she sometimes feared that Hildegard—her own beloved Hildegard—contributed to this flattening out of the literary landscape, to the slow death of the subtlety and ambiguity of meaning that always accompanied true human inspiration. That is, no true inspiration could be found in Hildegard's poetry, only lucky guesses at what inspiration might look like—and if this sham could fool a reader, then this was so much the worse. This inability to distinguish between the human and the virtual spelled the true death of human loftiness. "The stars are not wanted now," she said to herself, "put out every one; pack up the moon and dismantle the sun." The poem was nearly over now. Mona was almost at her stop.

Yet despite all that, the poem continued to exist. Not the way it had been intended, perhaps, but it existed just the same. It simply kept going on, in Mona's mind and in the minds of many others. Thus there was, Mona posited, some kind of independent force looking out for whatever might be inspired or transcendent in this world, whether literary or no, and she felt, at her brighter moments, that this force—in all its mystery and majesty—might be muffled or sent underground, but could never be utterly denied.

*

As soon as Mona made it out into the cold, quiet Roosevelt Island evening, her phone began to ring. The number was private. Natalie was the only person to whom Mona had given her digits, and if this was Natalie, Mona certainly did not want to talk to her. She walked quickly north along Main Road toward her home, letting the phone ring all the while. It was one of those evenings on which Roosevelt Island felt deserted. Not a soul in sight—only the whispers of little waves on the river rising and falling in the dark. She felt at this moment that it was an island somehow *built* to give a sense of desolation: rows of identical cement apartment complexes, wide empty lots expanding as one approached the roaring Queensboro Bridge, the exposure on all sides to a sharp, salty wind. And then there was the abjectness of her own little phone, bleating tinnily into air.

When she first moved, Mona had read of the prison that had served as the island's main attraction, and of course she'd learned that the Octagon, her home, had been an institution for the insane. But she'd never really let the substance of these facts infiltrate her consciousness, caught up as she'd been with her own private fears. Now, however, in the silence of the night, it seemed to Mona that her walk along the water's edge was nothing but a temporary stroll that led, and always would lead, back to her numbered cell. And indeed when she entered her condo Mona saw it had the anaesthetized look of a place one did not live in but to which one was confined.

She got into her unmade bed. The phone rang and rang.

And rang, as she drifted off, as though it were a white noise machine designed to lull insomniacs to sleep. In semiconsciousness, Mona's mind pieced together evidence: someone had been looking for Mona, yes. Or they had been looking for something Mona *had*. And yet she had nothing, no. And who were *they*? They were the man with the iPad, the man in the salmon fleece, and Jen and Jon, Natalie, Marcos. And Marcos led back to Jen and Jon. And Jen and Jon led to Natalie, who was dead. Dead dead. Dead why? Dead for what she knew. But Mona was not dead, no. No, Mona was not dead.

A knock came at the door. Initially Mona's dream state managed to contain the sound, subsuming it and letting it punctuate her staccato thoughts. But now it got loud and fast enough to jolt her awake. Her first conscious instinct was to dash to the window and hop out of it. But the apartment was twelve flights up and the windows only opened for the width of an ankle, anyway. Her next instinct was to stay under the covers until whoever it was got the sense that no one was home. But as soon as Mona had had this thought, her phone rang out loud and clear enough for anyone in the hallway to hear. She wondered why she had not put the stupid thing on silent. The phone was like Mona's own tell-tale heart—except that she had outsourced her conscience, or whatever it is that makes one miserable and aware, to a mechanical appendage.

The knocking began again, even harder than before. The tempo of its bass tones, steady and slow, kept time with the phone's manic filigree. Mona's comforter was thick and downy, but under it she nonetheless felt a chill, as though the wind had seeped in through her window and taken refuge in her sheets. She kept perfectly still. Into the darkness of the room a vague orange light filtered through: from the streetlamps below and from the lights of the office building across the river that are never extinguished. Mona closed her eyes and listened to the beating of her heart. The phone's melody had ended in the middle of a bar, and soon after that the knocking stopped, too. For a moment there was quiet.

Then someone called out Mona's name. She thought she recognized the voice, but in her state of fear everything seemed both familiar and strange.

"Mona," the voice called out again, "open up, I know you're in there."

"Del?" Mona said, "Del, is that you?"

"Of course it's me," Del said, "we had poetry hour scheduled for tonight. Don't tell me you forgot."

Mona's body relaxed as she heard the familiar, nasally voice. "I'm sleeping, Del," she said, "let's just postpone."

"Sleeping? For goodness sake it's only just after nine. And I've got some very important things to chat with you about. Come on, why don't you just throw on a nightgown and open up?"

Mona, who had never in her life owned a nightgown, was fully clothed in hoodie, Levi's, and wool socks under her comforter. She rose from bed and went to the door. In the fish-eye Del's pale face billowed as he moved it now closer, now farther away. Mona opened the door up a crack.

"Have you seen any men with salmon shirts tonight?" Mona asked.

"Not a one."

"Men with iPads?"

"Zippo. Nada."

"And no one has followed you here?"

"You seem tense, Mona. Have you been going to your Pilates classes?"

"I haven't had time. Listen—"

"Or doing any of those breathing exercises we talked about? Why don't we take a lion's breath together right now? Ready?"

"Del—"

Del crouched down, stuck out his tongue and exhaled deeply, in the manner of a roaring lion.

"Oh for God's sake," Mona said, "just come in."

*

Del had brought for discussion a "startlingly original" book of poetry, *Subject*, which had become a surprise bestseller that year. It was poetry primarily in the sense that it was difficult to parse and contained line breaks. The final third of the book was comprised of a long, discursive prose poem on the subject of subjectivity, throughout which the author's position on positionality was lovingly detailed. Mona read the praise on the front cover, back cover, and inside flap, and she felt very tired.

"*Subject* challenges you to decode half-hidden symbols of power... a book that deconstructs, in every sense of the word ... subverts the way words formulate power and the way power informs our words... fervently smashes complacency."

"I thought we might talk this evening," Del said, "about the relation of power structures to language."

"Why don't you educate me on the subject," Mona said, though she regretted it as soon as the words came out. "I'm too foggy to be of much use tonight, anyway."

Though Mona had flipped the light on once Del came in, certain features of the apartment retained the nightmarish aspects they'd taken on in the dark. Mona's dining table, for instance, seemed to have had its dimensions distorted since she'd last taken stock of it, and her wide glass windows were whistling a tad too loud in the wind.

"Well I wanted to talk," Del said, "about the fact that all our actions are informed by power relations and by violence."

The wind whipped through the dead branches of the cherry trees planted in rows beyond the parking lot outside Mona's building. The branches flickered under the lamplight and their shadows danced across the tar.

"And since words are, you know, speech acts," Del continued, "that means the words you use are formed by the violence that underpins the patriarchy. And they serve to reinforce it, too."

The fluorescent light above them twitched and fizzled, then resumed its bright silence. "Pretty heady stuff you've been reading," Mona said and sighed.

"Yes," Del said, "I think it is. But so given all that, my question is: how does a poet decide which words to use? How would *you* decide?"

Mona nearly roused herself out of the fog of the last several hours to answer. In fact, she felt for a moment—and it occurred to her how odd it was that this tended to happen just as one was nearest to despair—that she was suddenly near some special new insight. She had formulated, and was about to express the fact that language, of all the things in the world, is the one means by which we can remain free, despite the dull murderousness of the past which has formed us. That there is always some divine spark in language ready to transcend its function as mere tool for communication, so that it was absurd to think language would be weighed down by something as inconsequential as material reality. And Mona was almost at the point of connecting this thought to the work of Hildegard, which for all its cleverness as a program could do nothing of interest without the human imagination being fed to it in the form of the corpus of poems Mona had chosen. And she felt, just as she was on the verge of expressing this thought, that it also somehow connected with Parr's death—just as sometimes in a dream an abstract notion will bleed, disconcertingly, into a concrete, physical fact. *Del, I love you*, she nearly said aloud, *I think I'm about to figure it all out*. But just at that moment her phone rang again.

"Your phone's ringing," Del said.

Mona froze. She held her thumbs to her temples as the gossamer web of connected thoughts dissolved.

"Mona, your phone's ringing," Del said again.

"Thank you, Del," Mona said, "I am aware."

"Well are you going to pick it up?"

"I am not."

"Don't you even want to know who's calling?"

"Let's focus on poetry hour."

"If it was me," Del said, "I would want to know who's calling."

"If it *were* me," Mona scolded, "and if it's important to you, the fact is that the number's restricted."

"You know that without even looking. So this isn't the first time they've called."

"Power," Mona said, "you had wanted to talk about power. So let's talk about it. Now the thing is, that once we start attributing nefarious Machiavellian motives to everyone—literature and philosophy is only a way of buttressing power structures, let's say—well then what's to stop someone else from attributing the same sort of motives to *you*? Where is it that we got the pedestal from which to look down on everything so objectively, you know?"

The phone continued to ring. Del stared at it wistfully: he did not appear to have taken in a word of what Mona had just said.

"It's probably a telemarketer," Del offered finally, "you should pick up and tell them to put you on the Do Not Call list."

"I *really* don't think it's a telemarketer. Anyway—"

"You have to be very explicit with them. I worked as a telemarketer myself once. Even if you pick up and say you're not interested, they still put you on their list to be called back. It's called a 'soft no.' You've got to either say explicitly 'do not ever call me again' or swear at them. Then that's considered a 'hard no.'"

"Listen Del, it's not a telemarketer. Things have got very complicated lately. People are dying all around me—being murdered, I mean. I can't prove any of it, but it's true. First it was my boss, now it's this woman Natalie. For all I know I could be next. I know as much as Natalie did, anyway. Also, last night I fucked a sociopath who seems to have serious control issues, and he very well may be spying on us now as we speak. But the point is, I don't know how whoever it is found my number, but whatever they're calling about *cannot* be good, and I don't feel quite ready to deal with it just yet, so if we could *please* just try to ignore the phone for now...."

The ringing stopped. Mona took a deep breath in. The silence was the most delicious silence Mona had ever known. But then the phone made a supercilious little chiming noise.

"You got a text," Del said.

"You look at it," Mona said, "and tell me what it says."

"It says 'pick up your phone.' What's going on with you, Mona? Come to think of it, I thought you didn't even use a cell phone normally."

"I really don't have the energy to explain."

Another chime. Mona only grimaced. Del read out without emotion: "It says 'I know you are reading this, and I know you are home. Pick up now.'"

The two of them stood in silence under the bright fluorescent light. Another chime. "'Or you're a dead woman,'" Del read out. And at that moment it began to ring once more.

"I'm answering it," Del said.

"Don't," Mona said.

"You at least want to know who you're dealing with, then you can be more specific when you file a report."

"Don't," Mona repeated, and she reached out for the phone. But Del had already answered and pressed the speaker button so that they could both hear.

"Jesus Mary and Joseph," Detective Aldo's melodic voice spoke out into the room, "for a supposedly literary gal you don't go in much for communication. What happened to common courtesy? You mind dropping by my office at the soonest possible convenience? We've already got two dead bodies on our hands, and I've got a feeling if we don't talk soon we might have three."

PART THREE

From the Diary of Avram Parr

December 7, 2015

Thank God for Mona Veigh. I have had my *eureka* moment. They say the fulfillment of your deepest desire shall be found in the place you least wish to look. I now see the wisdom of this. It is not mystical mumbo jumbo, as I had previously supposed. Rather, it is a way of saying that one's greatest insights require a concentration of one's whole self. And if a part of the self is being ignored, because it is strange or frightening, or simply tedious, then such concentration of the will is impossible.

It should have been obvious to me. Language. What else but language would be the key?

What is the world of humans made up of if not of language? What else is at the core of each human life? And all because of Mona Veigh's infernal poetry....

My conversation with Mona yesterday afternoon started on the topic of neural networks. These synthetic systems are, of course, modeled on the structure of the human mind, and they have proved to be the most successful methods of artificial intelligence we have been able to construct. That they are inordinately powerful was no doubt apparent to Mona: her own program, Hildegard, was built using one.

Yet she was skeptical of the ability of neural nets to fully mimic the workings of the human mind. She said that there was a missing piece to the puzzle that researchers could not yet locate. And, as usual, she thought this had something to do with poetry. So we began discussing the ability of neural networks to learn language.

It was my fairly uncontroversial contention that every aspect of the human process of communicating could be mapped onto a decision tree; thus, this process could be re-created *in toto* by a neural net.

Mona maintained that this was not so. There was, in language, she claimed, something which we didn't yet have the wisdom to map.

"There are the words of a language," she said, "but there are also what a poet would call the spaces in between the words."

I told her that that sounded like the sort of elegant nonsense that literary people enjoy inventing simply in order to amuse themselves.

She glared at me for a moment, but I sense that by now she has learned not to take what I say personally, and to simply carry on with the elaboration of her ideas.

"Think of the way," she said, "words change their meaning over time. *Hanging out*, let's say, or *chilling*. These words would be mutually unintelligible to people from even one or two generations apart."

"Obviously those changes over time can be mapped," I said.

"Perhaps, but now think about it on a larger scale. Think of the statement 'I am left wing.' Well in the 1920s that could have meant you were a working-class follower of William Cullen Bryant and a racist to boot. In the 1960s it could have meant you wanted to drop out of society and do drugs. Now it might simply mean you want Medicare expanded. The words are the same. And we think we know what they mean. But the meaning has shifted under words that have remained the same. It turns out it's not actually the words that are of ultimate importance. But something writhing beneath them, struggling to get out. That's what a poet might mean by *the space between the words*."

I countered that, again, though these meanings which shift over time might be endlessly complex, they still might, theoretically, be mapped onto a neural network with sufficient layers and nodes, so that a computer could successfully parse them out.

Mona seemed exasperated. It was interesting to be on the other side of a conversation where one person simply cannot grasp the other's conception. I even felt a moment of sympathy for all the witless interlocutors I've disdained over the years.

"*Theoretically*," she said, "always with the *theoretically*. Something that is theoretically possible may very well be practically impossible. In fact it may become impossible just as soon as it's put in practice."

This was plainly true, and has been demonstrated by Gödel's Incompleteness Theorem.

Now I was intrigued.

"Think of it," Mona continued, "like an analog computer versus a digital computer. Sure, digital computers are great for giving an *approximate* version of whatever real-world territory they're trying to map. But since they're converting your data into binary, they're always losing just a little bit of the picture. They're describing an object in a way that might be a technically accurate, but may leave out what's most essential about it."

"And yet last time I checked," I said, "you invented an artificial intelligence program using a neural net. You did not invent an analog computer in order to represent reality as precisely as possible."

"No, but that's just it. What's interesting about Hildegard is that it *doesn't* simply try to represent some aspect of reality. Unlike most people working in AI, I wasn't trying to re-create some feature of the world that already exists. I was just feeding Hildegard lines of poetry and seeing what it would produce, if given a chance. And what it produced was, as far as I could tell, some aspect of the sublime. That is to say: real poetry. Hildegard acted more like a divining rod and less like a compass. I gave it the words, and it captured what's in between the words. At least that's how it seemed to me: I suppose I'm biased because I'm the one who entered in the text that Hildegard works with. Maybe the right way to put it is that Hildegard is simply a microcosm of my mind, the same way my mind is a microcosm of the world."

I was about to respond with a typical reaction, say: "That is medieval philosophy, try to stick to post-Renaissance science." But at that moment the insight occurred.

"If I understand you correctly," I said, "you are saying that Hildegard is a tool that takes an input, and gives an output that is endlessly satisfying to the user."

"Not just satisfying," Mona said, "but to me it can be poetic, numinous, fascinating. The user is the ink, and Hildegard writes the book."

I thanked Mona for the stimulating conversation and dashed home to my loft. Eureka! I had figured it out.

I had been wondering all this time how to escape the tyranny of public opinion. And I had always run up against the same problem: no one will give up his or her tiny shred of power in order to create a better system; and this is why their opinions cannot change. To politely ask a bureaucrat or a pundit or journalist to think differently is to politely ask a sovereign to abdicate his throne.

You cannot mold people's opinions by shoving new ideas down their throats. But you can let them create a story of their own imagining. You can encourage those fantasies, and eventually shape them. True persuasion, that is, must come from within. One cannot change a person's thoughts, only reverse their polarity. In order to hate, one must first know love. In order to know freedom, one must first know bondage. And in order to know life, one must first know death.

(13)

"I'm here," Mona said to Detective Aldo once she had reached his office, "but only because I've got nowhere else to turn. And I'm not saying a word until you've let me in on whatever your involvement was with Parr's death. I've got a new source, and he's provided me with hard evidence of an NYPD cover-up."

"Any chance your new source is a stocky fellow, dark hair, medium height and none too genial, who left you in the lurch at a crime scene earlier this evening?"

"You know I know Marcos."

"In the biblical sense, it would appear."

Aldo leant back in his chair and spoke with a wry smile. Yet Mona sensed he was not as calm as he was trying to seem. Deep bags showed under Aldo's eyes, and Mona got the distinct impression he had been sleeping in his office. His checkered collared shirt betrayed a Rorschach of coffee stains and billowed out untucked over the waist of his drab gray slacks.

"So I've got a whole invisible retinue of government spooks trailing me," Mona said. "Just peachy. I suppose it was your men who put the QR code in my apartment to scare me away from the case."

"Afraid I don't follow you."

"Sure you don't. Just like you don't follow me when I say that there's been a cover-up. Just like you don't follow me when I tell you that Avram Parr didn't kill himself."

"You're calling me a liar, then."

"Well aren't you?" Mona said.

Aldo sat up straight in his chair and winced, as though the question were too painful to consider. He folded and unfolded his hands several times, looking at Mona with entreating eyes, before he finally spoke.

"Are you familiar at all," he said, "with Paul's first letter to the Corinthians?"

Mona sighed. "Is that the one where he wrote home to mom asking for more pocket money," Mona said, "or the one that he sent to the wench back in Jerusalem, letting her know she was a grand old dame but it just wasn't going to work out?"

"I'm afraid," Aldo said, "that *those* two letters are decidedly noncanonical. No, First Corinthians is the one where he uttered the famous line 'I have become all things to all men, that I might by all means save some.' Now, only a decade or so before all this, St. Paul had been a Jewish fellow named Saul of Tarsus, who devoted himself to killing Christians on sight. So he knew a little something about the old switcharoo."

"Sounds like a guy who knew what side his bread was buttered on."

"Yes, perhaps he was. Let me put it to you this way, Mona: I'm a lawman, and the law is the law—but the law isn't everything. Meaning if you *really* want to follow the law, sometimes you've got to go ahead and break it. Sometimes a truthful man's going to have to lie, and a good man's going to have to commit evil."

"Detective Aldo, with all due respect, if you don't level with me soon, I'm going to have to walk out of here and take my chances with being murdered."

"I'm afraid you wouldn't be able to get out of here if you tried. Not until we've had our little talk, at least. You see, Mona, I have some folks above me in the pecking order who'd like to see you arraigned for the murder of Natalie Kulak."

Mona sat up straight in her chair and felt the muscles in her back twinge. She fixed her gaze not on Aldo but on the window behind him. Only darkness out on the street.

"Excuse me?" Mona said. "Why would anyone want to pin that on me?"

"Well, for one thing, you were the last person who had texted her—several times, I might add—before her death. For another thing, because she had written a note to herself on her phone that very morning that asked, simply, 'What to do about Mona Veigh?' And finally, there's the inconvenient fact that you were at the scene of the crime, and fled without saying a word to anyone."

"Fucking hell."

"Now the fact is, some of my colleagues think you might be following St. Paul's advice too closely. They think maybe you've been acting under the law just to win over those of us on the side of the law. Whereas when you're with those folks without the law—your friend Marcos, for example—then perhaps you act in an entirely different way, to win them over. Now I'm not one hundred percent convinced by this theory. If I was, then you would have gotten more than a phone call from me requesting your presence. I do need, however, for you to explain to me precisely what you've been up to since we last spoke."

Mona recounted everything—from the visit to her old office building to her afternoon to Marcos's allegations against Aldo to the crime scene outside WorkLife. And she found herself becoming increasingly angry as she did so. She was outraged by the lengths to which they had gone in order to cover up Parr's death and to torture her simply for trying to get to the truth. The sordidness, the indignity of it all. She repeated that word: *indignity*. She said that Parr may have been cold and strange but that he was a reasonably good employer and an intelligent person with ideas to contribute, and that he did not deserve to be murdered. And that's what this was, Mona found herself blurting out, a murder and a conspiracy that Aldo and his friends were perpetrating, and now to add to the indignity of it a person as kind and innocent as Natalie had been killed just to cover things up—and if Aldo was too blind or stupid to see all this, then that was his own problem.

"I suppose that would be my problem," Aldo said, "but as a matter of fact I know that Parr was murdered as well as you do."

"And another thing," Mona said. "Even if you didn't plant the QR code, which I don't quite believe, I don't see how it's very professional to go in cahoots with the NSA, or whatever the hell you did in order to get my number, and send threatening messages to my—wait, what did you say? You're admitting it?"

"Yes, I'm admitting it, but unfortunately the rest of what I'm about to tell you is not going to be so much of a relief."

Aldo tried to explain it as gently and patiently as he could. He began by asking Mona if she had ever heard of "regenokine procedures." She had not.

"It's the term for a new kind of high-tech blood transfusion," Aldo said. "I presume you are familiar with the array of biogenetics firms that Parr had purchased—Purusha and CRISPR-X, for example? CRISPR-X is where your friend Natalia worked before her 'promotion.'"

"I know that one, but I don't know Purusha."

"Well I'll just have to tell you all about it, in that case," Aldo said.

Purusha, it turned out, was a regenokine firm focused on increasing life expectancy through the transfusion of younger, healthier blood cells into older or diseased bodies. In this it did not differ so much from several other biomedical startups in Silicon Valley. Where Purusha did differ, though, was in the speed and the recklessness with which they pursued their venture. Because blood infusions are perfectly legal and FDA-approved, there was nothing stopping Purusha from pumping blood into and out of whatever bodies they pleased. So at the beginning, the company was in contact with legal, reputable blood banks to get a regular supply of fresh blood, while their clients, mostly wealthy people from in and around the Valley, paid large sums for transfusion procedures that were experimental at best.

This was Purusha's business model in the early days of its operation. Except that soon its customers began to complain that they weren't seeing the results they had hoped for. Some dreamers among them had signed up thinking they'd slap another fifty years of perfect health onto their once lusty lives and became enraged when they discovered they were still prone to everything from prostatitis to cold sores to terminal cancer.

Beyond that, the company was starting to run out of blood. Regulators began to wise up and wondered whether it was really all gravy to have nonprofit blood banks trading sacks of O-negative for cash with a for-profit research group that employed precisely zero practicing doctors. Meanwhile, Purusha's mandate from its overseers at Proserpina was to get results, to get them fast, and to bend whatever regulations might need to be bent. Parr had, in fact, made it clear to the head researcher at Purusha, a Dr. Shlomo Ross, that he had a two-year period in which to achieve the level of success Parr was looking for, or else Parr would pull his investment and look for the path to Shangri-la elsewhere.

At this point in the story Mona began to feel physically ill. But at the same time, she knew how things worked when big sums of money were on the line: standard practice was to act fast and justify one's actions to the law only after the fact.

"So Parr pressured a biotech company he purchased to act a tad unethically," Mona said. "I don't see what's so godawful about that."

"Yes, indeed," Aldo said. "I'm getting there."

What was so godawful was that in the months after Parr's ultimatum, Purusha's activities moved from the realm of mere shadiness to that of the starkly illegal. The company began secretly circulating—among young, healthy, low-income populations—the opportunity to take part in a bold new medical experiment. The exact nature of the experiment was not disclosed, though the $50,000 payment was printed clearly enough.

Volunteers would learn all about the *exciting* new procedure once they had made an in-person visit and passed their blood tests at Purusha's medical compound on the outskirts of Cupertino.

And in fact the new procedure was so exciting that it could have come straight out of a horror movie. The ineffectiveness of Purusha's prior experiments, it turned out, had not been due to any errors in their procedure or because the blood they'd harvested had not been young or fresh enough. Rather, it was because the customers' Notch signaling and satellite cells had failed to activate, due to degeneration of the serum over the course of transfer. That was the technical way of putting it. The simple way was that there needed to be less time between when the blood was circulating in the healthy young person's body and when it made it into the old person's veins. The solution, then, was evident: parabiosis, i.e. the actual stitching together of the two organisms, for a period of three days.

Parabiosis had been tested on mice up till the 1970s, after which point a creeping sense among medical professionals of the procedure's gruesomeness led to its being quietly abandoned. There was also the fact that a group of independent researchers in Denmark surmised a link between the procedure and the subsequent development in some mice of fatal orthokine diseases.

But Purusha pushed on regardless. The patients were sworn to secrecy. The customers were warned that the procedure would be a risk. The result—fantastically, unexpectedly—was a complete success. Purusha's Dr. Ross, like a modern-day Frankenstein, had sewn together separate human beings with delicacy, thoroughness, and tact. And over the course of their seventy-two-hour symbiosis he had them both thoroughly sedated, so that the nastiness of the procedure would only be preserved as a vestige of the unconscious, if at all. Then, a mere two weeks after they'd been cleared to go home from Purusha's lab, the customers began to feel that they really *had* found the elixir of life. For one of them, arthritic knee pain suddenly and permanently abated. For another, the scaly flakes of his psoriasis gave way to a smoothness of skin he hadn't known since childhood. Soon scores of elderly or infirm rich people were blocking out time for vague vacations on their Google Calendars and heading to Parr's medical lab on the bay.

At this point in the story Aldo paused. It seemed to Mona that he was taking stock of the effect his speech had had on her so far: his eyes were bloodshot and open wide, as though they'd just been dilated. He sat perfectly still, his features all but unanimated. Only a small, sour grimace appeared on his face as he continued on toward the story's crux.

"It was just a few months after the fact," Aldo said, "that blood started showing up in the urine and stool of certain blood donors. Then one of them developed hemarthrosis in his knee—which basically means that the joint had been destroyed. Another one, I'm sad to say, suffered a cranial hemorrhage while he was playing in his company's annual softball game, and died there on the field. You see, Mona, these donors had developed severe hemophilia. Their blood wouldn't clot properly, which means it was dangerously thin, down to 10,000 or so platelets per microliter. And let me tell you something—there are a lot of things you can have wrong with you and keep soldiering on with the help of a few pills and potions. But blood that's thin like that is not one of them."

Mona felt the force of Aldo's words slowly closing in on her, but she was not ready yet to let them permeate her mind.

"So," she said a bit breathlessly, "Parr was negligent about a biotech company he owned. Fine. And you think that means that he should be murdered? After all, whoever signed up for the procedure knew that it was experimental, no? Sometimes risk outweighs reward, and this turned out to be one of those cases."

"Yes," Aldo said, "it certainly did." His sad eyes looked out at Mona as if he were about to tell a credulous child that Santa Claus was a fraud. "If only that was the end of it."

But it was not. Because now Purusha, and thus its parent company Proserpina, had a legal problem to deal with. Not to mention the fact that nobody wanted to shut down a procedure that looked like the first big break in anti-aging technology.

So Parr offered the sick blood donors a proposition. They could stay quiet and double their money (nor would Parr be stingy with any medical bills that might need to be furtively paid)—or else they could find themselves in a heap of trouble. He didn't care to explain just what he meant by trouble. But he assumed they got the gist.

All but two of them did get the gist. Those two, however, a pair of brothers from McAlester, Oklahoma, who had a frontiersman sense of righteousness and a corresponding blindness to danger, told Parr that they would be going ahead and filing suit. Never mind that they'd be breaching the confidentiality agreement they'd signed. The two of them knew they'd been had, they knew this was just another case of arrogant schemers on the coast thinking they could do as they pleased and damn the consequences. The brothers didn't care for the money, they said, though one of them was out of work and the other earned a precarious biweekly check at a call center. What they cared about was exposing what Proserpina had done to them. They called Parr to make their intentions known, prepared a list of the top malfeasance lawyers in the area, and were found dead in a freak auto accident within the week. It appeared, the papers said, that they'd been killed in broad daylight, as they crossed the Main Street Bridge toward the creek where they were in the habit of walking their German Shepherd, Rosie. Rosie survived the attack with only minor injuries. The perpetrator was never found.

"I'm not seeing any proof Parr had them killed," Mona said.

She heard the words escape her mouth, but even as she said them she felt their hollowness.

"You're not, eh? Oh Mona, if only there really were no devils in the world—only careless drunks and earthquakes and slips on the ice. Then we wouldn't need cops, and I could go live in a monastery upstate and spend my days intoning the rosary and brewing porter. But no, for some reason Parr was more careless than usual with the Pendrick brothers. You see, he sent a text to your handsome friend Roland Marcos, whom we had been tracking for some time."

"Marcos," Mona said, "of course you bring him in."

"I'm afraid you can't pin that one on me. It was not I who brought Marcos in, that was the Guatemalan Civil War along with an increase in the number of H-1B visas granted under the Clinton administration. Brought in a whole lot of other fellows from Quetzaltenango, too. In any case—"

"Marcos said that he was Cuban."

"Marcos says a lot of things. A few of them might even turn out to be true, now and then, when you look at them under a certain light. One thing we can be plum certain of is that he relayed a message from Parr to two of his goons back in the spring of 2015 telling them to hightail it to McAlester. We can be so certain because we intercepted the text message from Parr, the subsequent message to the hoodlums, and tracked the purchase of two plane tickets from New York to Tulsa."

"So Marcos never really was a special agent?"

"Oh, he was special all right. Before he got cozy with Parr he did the bidding of all varieties of petty crime bosses. But you can bet your bell-bottoms any kind of badge he's ever had came from a novelty store. We've got quite the file on him, and on Parr too, as a matter of fact."

Aldo pulled a manila envelope out from a crate on his desk and waved it at her. "You'll find all the messages pertaining to the McAlester murder toward the back. Up front are detailed records of Purusha's reckless procedures. Toward the middle you'll find all the details of Parr's—what do the kids call it, Parr's *bromance* with Roland Marcos."

Mona began to read through the file, but after a while she found herself overcome by a peculiar difficulty in comprehending it all. It was as though she had developed an allergy to the printed word itself.

"No, it's not the most pleasant stuff, is it?" Aldo said. "Stitching folks together, leaving them high and dry with terrible diseases, murdering them when it's convenient. One wouldn't think that hit-and-run would be an effective method, in this age of mass surveillance. But if you've got fake plates and a couple of burner cars—well, it's not the most ingenious way to kill, but it does the job."

Mona froze in her chair. "Natalie," she said softly.

"Yes, Natalie. A terrible shame."

"But then," Mona said, "who called for that murder? And why?"

"That's precisely what I intend to find out. I would say more than likely it's someone within the Proserpina network, in league with Marcos. It could be the same people who murdered Parr. Some of the things Natalie and her colleagues were up to at CRISPR-X were rather grisly as well—though I doubt you want to hear about it."

"No," Mona said, "I certainly don't. In fact I'll be ducking out of all this entirely, if you don't mind. Good luck with the case."

"I'm afraid it's not so simple as that, Mona. For one thing, I'll need you to be in touch with me if Marcos tries to reach you. Or if you see anything suspicious on Roosevelt Island."

"You mean the man with the iPad or the man in the salmon fleece? So you do believe me about them, too."

"I do, now that it appears Marcos and his associates want something from you. And unfortunately, when they want something, it's usually something they're willing to kill for."

Hildegard 2.0's Ballad of the Absentee Uncle

O Uncle Saul, the human flute,
He plays wherever he goes:
A simple song, gets at the root
of everything he knows.

O Uncle Saul, some say he's mad
("there's one in every family"),
but I could never see what's bad
'bout saving men from calumny.

Yes Uncle Saul, the human storm:
he blows from town to town.
Anywhere the weather's warm,
He rains his wisdom down.

No Uncle Saul, he doesn't care
just how you style your dick:
"If you really wanna cut down there
A clean slice'll do the trick."

"But Uncle Saul, what of the rites?
You make such little use of 'em."
"That's true," he says, "but O, man's rights
are not bound by Jerusalem."

Strange Uncle Saul, he's still a Jew
but says there is no law—
just do to him as he'd to you
and see the light he saw.

So Uncle Saul's the human sign
of all that is to come,
when last are first, the seeing blind,
and wisest brothers dumb.

Still I wish he weren't always out
in Rome or Thessalonica:
O Uncle Saul, the human flute,
he never comes to Hanukkah!

(14)

A soft rain came down on 33rd Street. The west wind blew paper garbage across the pedestrian seating area toward Kmart. It was nearly 3:00 a.m. The night was as still and quiet as the scene of a crime.

Mona had refused Aldo's offer of a cab ride back to Roosevelt Island. She said that if she were to be murdered between here and there, then she would just have to take it on the chin. Her fear had dissolved the moment she stepped out onto the street. It had been absorbed into something more like despair.

Yet despair was not exactly the word. It was a vertiginous feeling—a feeling that all the chaos implicit in the world (including the chaos implicit in Mona's own mind) had now come into bloom. Mona embraced the feeling. She stood motionless in the rain. It seemed to her now that she could safely discard everything she had once cared deeply about. She could dispense with morals and ideals. Not that such things were *wrong*, per se. They merely seemed irrelevant. It seemed to her that they were only so many puffed up phrases. All our words to describe the world and what we ought to do in it were irrelevant to the pulsing heart of it—to the animal instincts for power and sex and violence, which now felt hot and wriggly beneath Mona's skin.

It occurred to her that an abstract concept like the one she had just devised can become inextricable with the sensuous details of daily life—that perhaps every abstraction had its concrete correspondent, and vice versa. She couldn't quite formulate this idea satisfactorily to herself, but she could taste it. The lamplight felt thick and chalky against her field of vision and on the surface of her tongue. The cool breeze was as pale as a corpse. Mona felt dizzy and intoxicated as the rain fell against her warm flesh. She let the fever of her thought break, and began to walk. She would walk crosstown to the tram and wait for the first morning ride to the island, hoping to pass as much degradation and malevolence as she could along the way.

Mona was sick over the new information she had acquired about Parr, but what affected her most was that she was also thrilled by it. It stirred something in her she could no longer hide from herself. It was not that she took any pleasure in the fact that murders had been committed. In fact, when she considered Natalie, or the Pendrick brothers, in their concrete existence, she felt a tremor that brought her dismayingly close to tears. But at the same time, it was exhilarating to know that her work, which only a few weeks ago seemed like the height of futility, had brought her so close to the nexus of life and death. This, after all, is what had made Parr something more than a mere cipher in her eyes. She had sensed it in the beginning—that he represented a blind force that was taking over the world. The force was not like that which motivated the hot-blooded imperialists and marauders who had brought whole nations to their knees in ages past. Those bygone purveyors of atrocities had been urged on at least by human passion, by the fiery tempers and lusts that had been immortalized by the poets, and could continue to be in the future. But the force behind Parr was cold and ahistorical. It took no real pleasure in conquest or glory. It let out no wild yawp of victory. Instead, it was like a virus, or a line of code in infinite loop, replicating itself for no other purpose than to have done so. It was a future in which all the passions had been eliminated in favor of icy knowledge. Even life could be snuffed out in the effort to apprehend truth.

On Broadway the marquees were lit up, but no one spilled into or out of the theaters. It was much too late at night for that—and yet somehow Mona had expected to see people there, jostling one another under the neon awnings, their blood warmed by nearness to spectacle. The closest approximation Mona could find was a little man encased in his glowing halal cart, picking his fingernails, listening to reggaeton. She stared at him for a moment too long. He looked back at her as though he would have liked to take off her clothes and strangle her. She quickened her pace. The raindrops fell only sparsely now, and on the horizon a purplish hint of sun rose up through the mist.

An inkling of death made Mona anxious to locate some physical representation of the horror she felt running through her bones. Once morning came it would be too late. On the corner of 41st she saw a man lying in rags on top of a metal grate. But as she approached, she found he was asleep, and even looked peaceful as he softly snored and twitched his chapped lips. Now that she felt ready to welcome danger, danger appeared to have fled. All the devils had migrated to her own mind. Mona would have welcomed a confrontation with any of the stooges who had been following her, any of Parr's henchmen, anyone who might put her at risk—but tonight, for the first time in days, she felt sure she was totally alone.

Across the street she spotted one of Times Square's few remaining sex shops and made her way toward the leather-clad mannequins on display in the window. She pushed through the doors and fixed her gaze on the proprietor, a pink-haired woman with bags under her eyes. The woman ignored her. Mona stomped past the entranceway toward the toys.

Here, she thought, here among the dildos and harnesses and jellies, here is an appropriate level of squalor. But almost immediately the effect the place had on her was to produce sadness. Eerily, no music played over the sound system, and the large fluorescent lights lining the ceiling tinged everything below with a sickly yellow. Mona shuffled over into the edible underwear aisle. A small, bald man in an oversized polo shirt stood rubbing the plastic casing of one of the products with his forefinger and thumb. He turned to look at her. Shame—shame and terror—flickered in his lifeless eyes before he put the item down, turned away, and marched out of the store. The little bell dinged. What am I looking for here? Mona asked herself. What am I running toward, what am I trying to escape?

As Mona left the store the sadness she had only glimpsed surged and threatened to overwhelm her. She could feel the sensation trying to express itself through tears, but she held them back as she made her way across Broadway. Pain gestured to her, but she would not respond. What pain? Whose? At that moment she could not say. But she knew that if she were to let it in it would be unending. It seemed to her—but this must be false, a whiff of madness in it—that her entire life had merely been a bulwark against this pain and that it was near now to breaking through. Her love of poetry, her anger, her delectation this evening at the thought of evil: these had only been bricks in the wall holding it back. She saw clearly now what her bond was with Parr, what had drawn her to him despite herself: that his defenses against the pain of life were as immutable and stifling as her own. But to build his defenses he had had to inflict so much more pain than he ever could have suffered. Mona saw in a flash Natalie's disfigured corpse and the corpses of the Pendrick brothers. She felt implicated by her desire, somehow still present, to rise to Parr's defense, and by her own clenching denial of the outside world. Mona tried to think of something else. It was all too much to bear.

But a succession of images had now been let loose in her mind, and she could not stanch their flow with entreaties. Inexplicably—idiotically, she thought to herself—she now had a vision of herself as a child of about ten years old. Unlike Mona's preferred image of her young self, the child was not immersed in a book. Instead, she was on a playground a few blocks from her old home in Queens. It was a small, inglorious playground with a yellow jungle gym and a metallic slide. The sun shone, and ten-year-old Mona made her way across the monkey bars, smiling. In her mind's eye Mona's adult self appeared on the scene and approached the girl. She had something to say to her but didn't know what. Something kind and comforting, perhaps just a warm hello. The adult Mona took quiet steps toward the child, who was facing away from her, swinging from bar to bar. She placed her hand softly on the child's shoulder. The child turned. As the child did so, the sun's brightness seemed to swell until it had enveloped the entire scene. And then against this brightness Mona could suddenly see the child's face—it was not warm and welcoming but disgusted, sneering, twisted in fury at the adult who had somehow betrayed her.

Mona shuddered out of her daydream and found herself paused in the middle of the street, while grim pedestrians stepped disapprovingly around her. She felt a last wave of sorrow swell and press against the wall in her heart she'd erected against it. The wall held fast.

Lamplight glistened against the wet asphalt. The rain had stopped. Mona observed that her body was trembling, although she did not quite feel the tremble. All her desire to walk through lurid midtown had been extinguished, and she hailed a cab back to her lonely home.

*

Mona banged on Del's door. It was now 4:42 a.m.

"Poetry hour!" she shouted, "open up! We're doing poetry hour early this week. Rise and shine."

After a few minutes Del opened the door. The abjectness of his solitary life seemed more evident with his hair mussed and bags under his eyes.

"Mona," he said, "really?"

"It's poetry hour," Mona said, and she let herself in. Lotion and leftover bibimbap were set next to each other on the dirty glass coffee table. An old movie played on the television: two grown men riding a Ferris wheel together in noirish black and white. Mona shivered as she stood beside the couch.

"Are you OK?"

"The world is an evil place," Mona said, "only poetry hour is safe."

"I'm going to take that as a 'no.'"

"Only poetry hour is real," Mona said. "The world is a fraud. It is ugly and covered in blood and it reeks of death."

"You look like you haven't slept."

"The last dactylic foot of a line of hexameter may be substituted with two long stresses. The *Lyrical Ballads* were first published in 1798. There are people who believe that the whole world itself is just a long poem, ritually chanted. I'm sure I've read that somewhere."

The central air gurgled. Del shifted his weight. "Do you want to sit?" he asked.

"Yes," Mona continued, "all the world is just one long poem. We're just the syllables spoken by a creature we don't understand, in an alien tongue, and now and again the lines repeat. That is what is happening when we find ourselves in the same situation over and over. Now and again we find ourselves split open by a caesura, or uncomfortably enjambed. But none of it really matters. It feels like good or evil, love or hatred, life or death. But it is all just a stream of sounds, morally neutral, flowing on and on. I wonder if it will ever end."

"I can heat you up some bibimbap," Del said.

Mona looked at his tired, pale face. Its creases brought her back down to earth. He seemed so touchingly alive, so pitiable. Finally, a few tears dribbled down Mona's cheeks. She could never understand Del's naive equanimity, but she could be touched by it.

"Why did you first start coming to poetry hour?" Mona asked. "What was the point of it for you?"

"I don't know," Del said. "I always *liked* the idea of poetry. It seemed like a good path toward understanding more about beauty, or the sublime, or something like that."

"Well it's not," Mona said. "It's a form of madness cultivated by the morbid and the permanently deranged."

"I think you should get some rest," Del said.

Mona agreed. She apologized for her intrusion and left his studio, closing the door softly behind her on the way out. But she did not go back to her own room. The manic lucidity that sometimes accompanies sleeplessness spurred her on down the stairs and outside into the cool air of the island at daybreak. She felt that something important was still to happen before the sun rose all the way. Instinctively she walked north, toward the tech campus.

Taxis hummed along the Queensboro Bridge above her. Gulls circled its steel suspension bars. Mona turned from the road on the Manhattan side of the island toward the campus buildings and the ascending sun. The latter had emerged from behind an artificial knoll built by the landscape architects who had designed the site. Mona wended her way thoughtlessly along the gray gravel footpath. Like so many other *innovative* things, the campus buildings that flanked her were glassy and asymmetrical. Their shadows extended along the crushed stone of the walkway up onto the knoll's manicured grass.

Mona didn't know quite how, but the certainty that she was being followed returned to her. It was a relief, in a way. She felt the cool breeze tickle her skin as she strode toward the river and breathed in the salty air.

"Come out, come out, wherever you are!" she shouted. She laughed and shouted again into the nothing of the desolate air. And then she stopped. In one of the prefab glass panels of the Innovation Institute she spotted the reflection of a figure that was not her own. It had been there. She was sure. This was not a matter of an unsteady mind weaving together images out of its own fancy. At least that is what she told herself.

"Who are you?" she shouted.

The silence in response goaded Mona on. She stepped quickly toward the panel where she had seen the image—it was on one of the building's out-jutting curves. The figure was gone, but now Mona heard footsteps. She followed their sound around the bend and saw a tall, thin figure speed-walking away from her. The outline of the man sparked something terrible in Mona's imagination, but she wasn't sure exactly what. She knew she had seen this figure before—perhaps he had been among the stooges who had been following her. But that was not quite right. Rather, she felt he had been among the shadowy figures who haunted the dark places of her mind.

"Who are you?" she called out again, but he did not turn. He began jogging now in the direction of the knoll. She tried to run after him but felt her legs inexplicably heavy, as in a nightmare.

"If you want something from me, take it!" Mona called out. "If you want to kill me, then kill me already. For God's sake just tell me what you want!"

The man broke into a full run. He made his way over the knoll and beyond it, nearly at the water's edge. But before he had sunk entirely out of sight, he turned his head back in Mona's direction—and she saw staring out toward her the cold green eyes of Avram Parr.

(15)

"There is such a thing as cryogenics," Mona said. "There is such a thing as reanimation. I've seen it in movies. You zap the dead body back to life."

"There is also such a thing," Aldo said, "as people who have been under an unbearable amount of stress, who haven't slept in damn near twenty-four hours and who then see things that aren't really there."

Aldo seemed, in his dry and preoccupied way, relieved to have found Mona back in his office. He offered her a coffee from the Keurig machine and mixed in the half-and-half for her. His tired face was marred with crow's feet that ranged out onto the flesh of his puffy cheeks.

Mona had come to believe by this point that Aldo simply slept on a mattress of bankers boxes in his office.

"It's odd," she said, "it was like in a dream. His face didn't seem to be completely his. And yet it was him. Unquestionably. His gaze was his. His aura, or whatever one wants to call it."

"And his aura or whatever one wants to call it," Aldo said, "dissolved along with his body down into the grassy knoll?"

"Yes, exactly," Mona said, "except I can't say for certain whether Parr dissolved into the *knoll*. By the time I had climbed it and caught up to where he had been when he turned back to look at me, the body was simply gone. Perhaps he dove from there into the river."

"Yes, perhaps," Aldo said and rolled his eyes. "And did you see anyone splashing around there?"

"No, but maybe he has gills and stayed under. Maybe there is an East River Atlantis that we don't know about, and Parr is ruling over it right now as we speak."

"If I had been you," Aldo said, "I really would've taken me up on that cab ride and gone straight to bed."

Mona would in fact have finally gone to sleep once she'd returned to the Octagon from the tech campus, agitated though she'd been at the time. But it turned out there was a matter to attend to concerning Del. Mona returned early that morning to find that his door had been left ajar, while he himself seemed to have vanished. She called him and received no answer. Then she phoned Aldo to report the disappearance, only to find out that Del was safe and sound—relatively speaking—in the custody of the police.

It turned out to have been a rather comic situation, at least from Aldo's telling of it. Del, who that morning had opened his door cordially to a pair of unannounced guests, became sullen upon learning that they were detectives in plainclothes and demanded to be read his Miranda rights. They told him that he was not in fact under arrest and thus it was not their legal duty to read him anything. They did, however, ask him if he would be willing to answer a few questions about certain strange occurrences on Roosevelt Island. But Del remained silent. His guests informed him that really things would be much simpler if only he'd open up a bit. At which point Del launched into a disquisition on the history of police brutality in the twentieth century. He became so worked up, in fact, that he sprayed the shoes of one of the detectives with his spittle. The detectives, now having great fun, cited Del and his loose phlegm on an obscure public hygiene law, read him the rights he had previously demanded, and took him in to the station. Del was now sitting in a holding pen around the corner from Aldo's office. He had become much more talkative since his change of scenery, though it only took the detectives a few minutes to clear him of any possible wrongdoing.

All the same, they kept him in the cage with some other offenders and told him mockingly that he would likely be out within the month.

"Really," Aldo said, "my boys had a fine time with him. Tell him we'd all love a roundtable discussion with him on the constitutionality of a legal procedure of his choosing. Maybe we can go over *Roper v. Simmons*. For now, though, I'd like you to take him home. And for the sake of all that's holy, accept the cab this time."

"You don't want to come check out the knoll?" Mona asked.

"I want you to come with me to take your friend home," Aldo said, "and then we'll all have some rest. And then we'll discuss."

*

Mona and Aldo approached the holding pen. Del looked glum. He was flanked on both sides by men who were much larger than him, men who did not wear glasses or take an interest in poetry. Del's belt had been taken, and he kept his thumbs in his belt loops to prevent his khaki shorts from dropping down off his scrawny waist.

"What are you in for?" Mona joked.

"Funny," Del grumbled.

"Your friend is what we call a reformer," Aldo said, "like Savonarola, or Martin Luther. They were men of principle, men in whom the presence of the Holy Spirit was strong. But they were men who had to take care they did not choke to death on their own holiness."

"Are you going to get me out of here?" Del said.

"Sometimes," Aldo said, "it is simpler to tell the Holy Spirit, 'down boy,' and to just adhere to the law."

"I've never been to a prison before," Mona said. "Is this technically a prison?"

"It's a holding pen," Aldo said. "Not quite the same thing."

"I'd like to be let out of this cage now," Del said, "if nobody minds too much."

The men around Del were beginning to smile. Mona got the sense this was not the first time they had found him to be an object of amusement.

"Yes," Aldo said, "sometimes the reformer is brought before the courts and detained, or exiled, or sometimes, worse."

"I suppose I should feel lucky," Del said, "that your goons didn't break my neck, if that's what you're saying."

"It can be worse," Aldo said, "yes, for the true reformer, it can always be worse."

*

In the cab Del sat as far away from Mona as possible, with his head turned away from her toward his open window. It had become a brilliant, sunny day. Mona closed her eyes and watched little streaks of light float across the backs of her eyelids.

"Were they really so rough on you?" she asked.

Del merely grunted.

"I wish Aldo had told me he wanted you in for questioning. I would have told him to have his men take it easy on you."

"He's a friend of yours, then?"

"I was appalled by him when we first met," Mona said, "he has a pastel portrait of the Virgin on his desk, and framed pictures of his chubby-cheeked children. But now I guess I've come to like him. It's an odd feeling. I wouldn't mind being rid of it, but at present it just can't be helped."

Del took in a deep breath of air. His hand seemed to be shaking, and the very angle of his body, crookedly positioned toward the window, spoke with an articulateness that Del's words seldom reached. Mona tried to meet his eyes as their cab rolled slowly up the hill onto wide-berthed Park, but he kept them away from her, directing them instead toward the wider world.

"Anyhow," Mona said, "sorry for my meltdown the other night. Have you started in on the Shakespeare? We could do a real poetry hour tomorrow. It might help take our minds off things."

"Actually," Del said, but then he let his sentence trail off.

"Actually?" Mona said.

"I think maybe we should give poetry night a rest for a while."

Outside, the sun-bleached city shone in Technicolor: every hue seemed to have taken on an extra sharpness since Mona last took account of her surroundings. She was surprised to notice, for instance, the lurid pink of chrysanthemums bunched together on either side of a bench on one of Park's dreary traffic islands.

"Oh?" was all Mona said.

"Listen, it was thoughtful of you to want to share your love of poetry. But I think it's just a tad . . ."

Del finally turned to face Mona and puckered up his face as though he was on the verge of tears.

". . . self-indulgent. Analyzing these little details of rhyme and meter, when there's so much injustice in the world, so much going on. It's kind of like missing the forest for the trees."

Mona said nothing. She had half-expected this. In a way she was relieved. Poetry could, once more, become entirely private. Perhaps in the end one should not share one's love, just as it's so often fruitless to share a dream. Mona steered the conversation back to Del's arrest, a subject to which she knew he was eager to return.

"What were they grilling you about in there anyway?"

"They were asking me all sorts of stupid questions. And being incredibly aggressive and impolite. Mostly they wanted to know about the man I saw in our apartment building, the one in the salmon fleece."

"Our mystery man," Mona said gravely. "Tell me about him again. I've got a hunch now that he might hold the key to things."

"All I know is that I'd seen him around a few other times from afar. Then last week I saw him coming out of your apartment, though I didn't get a good look at his face. All I did notice were those strange hands, as he was turning the knob. One of his fingers, his ring finger maybe, was like freakishly longer than the others."

Mona felt her chest clench. She gripped the cabbie's seat in front of her to steady herself as she remembered the story Natalie had told her.

"Repeat that," Mona said.

"His ring finger. It was weirdly long. What, is that some important detail? I thought I'd mentioned that."

"No," Mona said, "that you had failed to mention."

And so the two of them sat in silence as the cab ferried them back over the river to their island outpost, never again to share a poetry hour. Over the next few weeks, Del would root out all the Oxford editions of Wyatt and Marlowe and Walter Raleigh that Mona had lent him, ringing the doorbell and sheepishly expressing gratitude for the loan. Mona, in turn, would return the various household items she had borrowed from Del simply by depositing them outside his door. These included a tape measurer, a humidifier, a pamphlet from the Rosa Luxemburg Society ("Of Foxes and Chickens: Oligarchy and Global Power..."), and a recipe book for cooking with soy. The one item she decided to hold on to for the time being was his knife.

*

Mona slept for what felt like days. In fact it was eighteen hours—she'd fallen asleep in the early afternoon, as soon as she'd walked through the door, and now it was the next day's dawn. Her sleep had been troubled, and she awakened with an abstract sense of impending doom, though she could recall only the faintest trace of a dream. Whatever vast landscapes of meaning spread out before her while she slept had now been dispersed by the cold logic of waking life. All that remained was a single, distant-seeming image: a faded rose against a background of pale blue sky. Mona tried to sharpen the focus of it, but the light creeping in from around her curtains beckoned to her. She opened them up to reveal a calm, bright morning.

She lumbered over to her marble countertop in a state of dejection and brewed her coffee. Mona was not satisfied with the idea that Parr's presence had been an apparition. The pale green eyes could not have been anyone else's. Then there was the matter of the man in the salmon fleece's finger. A mosquito hummed around Mona's neck—a last refugee from summer. She swiveled around on her barstool slowly, watchfully. The mosquito hovered before her face, mocking her. And it was only once she had squashed it, spraying the frail thing's blood onto her pale palm, that the idea came to her.

Mona hopped up from the barstool and pulled out her phone. She read over the list Jen Rostow had given her:

> Toya Clay
> Chief Medical Examiner
> tclay@ocme.nyc.gov
> 212-487-1351
>
> Mark Rollins
> First Deputy to the Chief Medical Examiner
> mrollins@ocme.nyc.gov
> 212-487-2335
>
> Detective Jerry Aldo
> 212-229-1968 [ext 42]
> Midtown Precinct South
> 357 W. 35th Street, New York, NY 10001

And she looked back over the mystery name she had unearthed from the document history of the link Jen had sent her:

> Christian Rosecrans
> Hematology
> 822-0929

She had gotten ahold of Aldo, of course. She had eventually reached the Office of the Chief Medical Examiner and spoken to a secretary, who had confirmed both Clay and Rollins as employees who had examined Parr's corpse. But Rosecrans had remained unknown. Mona mouthed the words out loud to herself over and over. Hematology: the study of blood. Parr *had* said, after all, that he was working on developing a sense of humor. Mona Googled through the history of Purusha's clinical trials, and found they had been advertised exclusively in small Midwestern towns, presumably so that they would not receive national notice. She made a list of the towns and found out their area codes. Then she tried each of the codes in front of Christian Rosecrans's number from the Google doc. The first attempt gave only the screeching sound of a disconnected line. The second went to the voicemail of a motorcycle shop. The third attempt, using an area code for Southwestern Missouri, was picked up after the first ring.

"Hello," a voice said.

"Uh, hello," Mona said. "Is this number associated with a hematology department, or in any way with the Office of the Chief Medical Examiner in New York?"

"Is it what?" The voice belonged to a woman who seemed both aggrieved and eager to speak. "The Office of the Chief Medical *who*"

Mona tried another tack. "Do you know how I could get in touch with a Mr. Christian Rosecrans?" she asked.

There was a pause. Mona could hear the woman's heavy breathing.

"Is this some kinda bullshit?" the woman asked. "Because I just got done a ten-hour shift, and if this is some kinda bullshit—"

"It's not," Mona said, "I'd like to speak with Christian Rosecrans. Please. Or to anyone who could put me in touch with him."

"Well Chris is dead," the woman said, "he died nine months ago. So that's gonna make speaking to him a little difficult."

"I'm very sorry to hear that," Mona said after a pause. "Are you a relation of Chris's?"

"Well first off," the woman said, "who the hell are you?"

"My name is Eva," Mona said, feeling her confidence rise with this first lie. "I'm an old friend of Chris's, but we hadn't spoken for a very long time."

"Seems like most folks hadn't spoken to Chris in a very long time. God knows I hadn't. My name's Annalisa, by the way. I'm Chris's cousin. How did you know him?"

"From work," Mona said.

"Ah," Annalisa said, "great. Another weed farmer."

Mona scanned her mind for any facts she might know about the farming of weed. None alighted. Luckily Annalisa continued on:

"You were a picker, too?"

"That's right," Mona said, "a picker."

"Was it really as tough as all that? I only heard from Chris once about it, and he talked about it like it was some kinda prison labor."

"It wasn't easy," Mona said, "no, it certainly wasn't easy. After a while one's hands began to hurt—from all the picking."

Mona cringed as she spoke. But she got the sense that Annalisa was already prepared to unburden herself.

"I wish he'd never gone off to California," Annalisa said. "That place does things to people. And Chris was so impressionable. He was so easy to lead this way and that, so when Misty and Pat and Gomer and them all said they were gonna strike it rich out on the coast, well then he couldn't but pack off with them in their junky old Subaru, and—"

"If you don't mind my asking," Mona interrupted, "how did Chris die?"

"Oh," Annalisa said. "God. God, it was awful. A terrible thing. Nobody really understands it, even now. After Chris had gone AWOL from the farm, nobody really knew what he was up to, or even how he was getting by. Then I guess he went and fell in with the wrong crowd, you know. Like I said, Chris could get swept up in things—didn't matter if they were smart or stupid. But all that said, I still have a hard time believing he was using. Heroin, I mean. But the doctors said it woulda only been from sharing needles that you get such a crazy blood disease—"

"Blood disease?" Mona said. She nearly shouted it. Her pulse was racing.

"Oh it was awful," Annalisa said. "When I saw the body, Chris hardly even looked like himself, he was so wasted and twisted up. He didn't even get a proper burial. The doctors said the disease was so strange and rare and all that, that they wanted to transfer him to a special hospital where the body could be used for science. Chris's parents objected at first, but then they got word there could be money in it for them—"

"Can I ask you a sort of odd question?" Mona said. And before Annalisa had time to speak, Mona continued:

"What color were Chris's eyes?"

"What color were his *eyes*? Didn't you know him?"

"I knew him," Mona said, "but the memory is fading. I was hoping you could bring him back to life for me."

The woman paused, considering this, before giving in to her emotions and choking out the words, her voice cracking and halting as she spoke:

"Honestly I sometimes come close to forgetting things about Chris, too. Just little things—the way he laughed, the way he scratched his chin when he was nervous. Anyway, his eyes were green, a beautiful pale green, but I don't see what that has to do—"

(16)

Mona hung up the phone. She threw on some clothes and hurried out into the street toward the subway. Down the long, long escalator to the F train the light got dimmer, and Mona turned for a moment to watch the above-ground world slowly recede. On the train, a man whose bulbous red, oozy face appeared to have been disfigured by an acid attack went from car to car singing R & B classics, asking for change. The woman across from Mona hugged to her chest a tote bag emblazoned with the phrases: EAT SMART, EXERCISE, ENJOY EACH DAY, RELAX, LIVE WELL, GET A WORK-OUT BUDDY, WALK 10,000 STEPS, BREATHE, DON'T SWEAT THE SMALL STUFF. Beside her, a teenage girl was removing her false eyelashes with miniature tongs.

From West 4th Street Mona strode to the WorkLife station. Its large glass doors glittered in the sun. Mona pressed the buzzer but received no answer. She rapped hard against the glass and pressed the buzzer again. A figure finally emerged. It was Jen Rostov.

Mona saw that Jen, upon making out Mona's features through the glass door, flinched and expressed half a movement back toward where she'd come from. But Jen caught herself, pasted on a smile and let Mona inside.

"Well if it isn't a total blast from the past," Jen said. "Actually, a little birdie told me that the cat might drag you back in one of these days. What's goin' down?"

"I want to talk to Avram Parr," Mona said.

There was a short silence, after which Jen laughed in a way that resembled the sound of a cat spitting up.

"Well," Jen said, "I *did* just buy myself a tarot deck, and I consider myself an enthusiast of the spiritual. . . but resurrection from the dead is still too tough a nut for me to swallow."

"Whatever you just said, I'm going to ignore," Mona replied, "and I'll repeat myself. I want to talk with Parr."

At that moment Marcos walked out of the bathroom. He nearly made it to the couch on the other side of the room, on which a large iPad was placed, before he noticed Mona.

"Delightful to see you again," Marcos said, but this time he did not smile his wide, empty smile.

"I'm less than delighted," Mona said, "but I might be something like appeased if you tell me how I can get in touch with Parr."

"What is she talking about?" Marcos said to Jen.

"I don't have time for this," Mona said. "I'll put it this way: man with the iPad, if you see the man in the salmon fleece, tell him to give me a ring. And remember: Parr and I were friends—in a manner of speaking. I think he owes me at least a conversation."

And with that she walked out the door.

It was peaceful and dusk in the Village. Mona began to walk uptown in the direction of her old office building, but she'd only gotten a few blocks when her phone rang. It was Aldo.

"I did some research on the tech campus at Roosevelt Island," he said. "Quite the place. I get the sense they're breeding a whole nother kind of human up there—biochips screwed into everyone's head, Wi-Fi receptivity in every newborn's fingertips, all that stuff."

"Things are moving very quickly." Mona said. "I'm going to need you to keep it succinct."

"Well," Aldo said, "about that knoll you said Parr, or the fella who looked like him, disappeared into. . . . Turns out you're not such a madwoman after all. See, in addition to the rest of their labs on the island, they've got an itsy-bitsy little nuclear fission program, which happens to be housed underground right around that knoll. The university muckety-mucks don't want it to be too public-facing, what with the deformed babies and radioactive potatoes and all that other fun stuff nuclear has associated with it. But the reactor's there all right—along with equipment and lab rooms for a few other companies the university officials don't want to broadcast out to the world."

"Name them," Mona said.

"Purusha and CRISPR-X."

"What a coincidence."

"Indeed. So what do you say we take a ride together to the Office of the Chief Medical Examiner this afternoon? I told them I'd be coming by with a trainee. We can ask a few extra questions about Parr's death. I'll have a car pick you up."

Mona was almost disappointed that Aldo was on the right trail, and was close to figuring out by his own method what she'd already discovered by dreams and intuition. But she thought she'd humor him and tag along. The one thing she wanted now was to get to Avram Parr, and maybe someone at the OCME would be able to give her a clue.

*

The office was not, as Mona would have imagined, a cavernous basement space filled with the rank smell of formaldehyde. Instead it was a semi-sleek brick and glass building near New York's main hospital complex, on 1st Avenue and 26th Street. Mona and Aldo rode up the slow elevator in silence.

As soon as the doors opened the two of them were greeted by an extremely efficient-looking woman in a lab coat.

"You must be Detective Aldo," she said, "and you must be Mona Veigh. We're always pleased to assist our municipal colleagues in law enforcement. I'm Dr. Toya Clay, the chief pathologist here at Bellevue OCME. Come right this way."

She escorted them down a long corridor. Mona could hear Aldo beginning to breathe heavily. Dr. Clay declaimed as they walked:

"I should inform you," she said, "that I personally examined Avram Parr's body and I can assure you both that the investigation was executed with utmost thoroughness. I've been doing this work for twenty-eight years now, twenty-nine in December. However, I'm prepared to answer any questions you may have. As I said, we especially welcome teamwork with our municipal colleagues."

She cracked her knuckles at the end of her speech. "Well, I do appreciate that," Aldo wheezed.

They reached a bright, spacious conference room and sat down around an oval table.

"I was just hoping," Aldo said, and he continued to cough and even hack up phlegm into his handkerchief, "I was just hoping—and I do appreciate your taking the time out to chat with us—that you could walk us through exactly what happened on the night of Avram Parr's death. Anything you can share that might not have shown up in the autopsy report."

Dr. Clay folded her hands together and smiled with bright annoyance.

"It was a perfectly run-of-the-mill case. A phone call came in from a friend of the decedent—"

"The decedent?" Mona said.

"The deceased. The dead. Avram Parr's corpse. A phone call came in from the person who found the body—"

"And that was?" Mona asked, though she could guess the answer.

"A colleague. Her name was Jen Rostov. She hadn't heard from the decedent for an unreasonable length of time, so she let herself into his apartment. She was in possession of an extra pair of keys."

"Of course she was," Mona said.

Dr. Clay glared at her and drummed her fingers on the desk.

"In any case, the BCPRT traveled to the decedent's place of residence." This time Aldo interrupted her.

"Gonna have to unpack that one, doc."

"Body Collection Point Recovery Team," she sighed. "It consists of OCME personnel whose job it is to retrieve the decedent at the Body Collection Point. They then transport the body to the nearest Borough OCME office or off-site morgue. In this case, the nearest location was this very building. A few flights downstairs is the site of our DEF—that is, Decedent Examination Facility."

"And how was the body identified?" Aldo asked.

"Generally, a family member will enter the premises to identify the decedent's face. But in this case, the decedent had no close family members local to the area, so two colleagues were contacted: Jen Rostov, the same young woman who had notified the authorities about the decedent, and another colleague named Roland Marcos."

Mona smiled. Aldo coughed a few more times.

"And it's only on the word of these two... colleagues," he asked, "that it was decided that the, erm, decedent—the corpse, I mean—that it was in fact Avram Parr?"

Dr. Clay cleared her throat, as though she was trying to shame a noisy theater patron or someone who had caused a disturbance at church.

"I must admit," she said, "that you've asked a rather odd question. To begin with, surely you're aware that Avram Parr was something of a public figure. The idea that he could be misidentified—well, I'm simply not quite certain how to respond. Beyond that, however, it so happens that Mr. Parr participated in the NYC DNA Registry Project a half a decade ago—and so a sample was taken of the decedent to match the DNA we had for him on file, just as a matter of procedure. I also do remember that the two colleagues who confirmed the decedent identified a wound on his left ring finger that he had recently incurred, I believe they said, while chopping vegetables. No doubt others who were in contact with the decedent at the time could confirm."

"No doubt," Mona said, and got up from her chair, "the body was cremated, correct?"

"That is in the affirmative," said Dr. Clay.

"One last question," Mona said. "As far as you know, has anyone ever worked here by the name of Christian Rosecrans? A contact of mine listed him as an employee of the OCME, but I think it may have been a mistake."

"No one by that name has ever worked here," Dr. Clay said. "I'm the head pathologist here and very cognizant of my surroundings. If there had been such a person, I would have known."

*

"Who's Christian Rosecrans?" Aldo asked in the elevator on the way down.

"Just another casualty," Mona said. "He's the poor schmuck who signed up for Purusha's trial run and ended up being murdered and express shipped to New York to fill in for Parr's corpse. Parr's people at CRISPR-X must have searched far and wide for someone who bore a resemblance to him. But my guess is that it goes even deeper than that, and they found a way to alter Rosecrans's genome so that the DNA sample they took from his body looked like it could have been Parr's, and that way they fooled the medical examiner. Jen accidentally led me to Rosecrans's trail when she shared a little document with me—I guess she didn't think I had it in me to put the pieces together."

"You had the scoop on me this whole time," Aldo said. "My golly. And to think I ever doubted you. You ever think of joining law enforcement?"

"After this, I've had enough crime and punishment for one lifetime," Mona said. "Now I just want this all to be over. But for it really to end, I'll need to talk to Parr."

"You may be the only one who can," Aldo said. "He might still trust you. He may even still be fond of you, for all we know."

"For all we know."

She parted ways with Aldo and headed back to Roosevelt Island. She was a mile high in the tram, suspended between the glittering city behind her and the peace of her drab island up ahead, when a disturbing thought entered her mind. The sun had begun to set and the faces of the crowd on 2nd Avenue receded from view, their features becoming indistinguishable from one another as the tram arced higher and higher, vying now with the glass towers of York Avenue for ascendency. Mona wondered how many humans had fallen from this height simply in order to construct trams or bridges or all the other modes of transport we take for granted. Or how many had fallen from towers from this height, their bodies cutting a jagged path through the wind until their features became indistinct, like those of the rest of the crowd at ground level, until they became nothing but a speck. And then splat: the speck would become a little splotch.

She had been repulsed by the information Aldo had given her about Parr's crimes. Yet how many splotches had she and Aldo stepped over without even knowing it, simply walking down the street? How many splotches had splattered in factories, in laboratories, on the battlefield? Was that not how civilization worked? What right did she have to feel disgust, when so many massacres, out of sight and out of mind, had laid the groundwork for the comfortable life she now enjoyed? How could one pick and choose?

As the tram glided smoothly over the river, leaving the faces of the crowd even farther behind, an even more extreme version of the thought twisted its way into Mona's head. Who was she to say that such deaths were bad in the grand scheme of things—all that was truly beautiful or worthwhile was something that had to be fought for, had to be risked. Our greatest innovations all entailed their share of splat. Mona stood up so that she could keep her eyes trained on the shrinking island she was now departing, and tried to follow the path of one single pedestrian for as long she could, before he diminished into nothingness.

She had just lost sight of this last human soul when she received a call on her cell from a restricted number. Mona answered the phone.

"Read any good poems lately?" the voice said.

Hildegard 2.0's Marriage of Heaven and Hell

Sunset is the color of murder,
White is the face of the dead.
Push your desire a bit further
And you'll see that blood is not red—

But black, like the black of a raven
And thick as a jam made from scratch.
Love is a tender young maiden
Locked in her mores with a latch.

But when the latch breaks it's a chaos
And love and hate mingle as one,
And a knife to the throat suits a lover
As well as a day in the sun.

Softly, softly, the weeping
Of sick souls fills heaven with tears;
In Hell all the heroes are sleeping:
They dream of mortal man's fears.

But earth is the place for confusion—
Let impulse pull each his own way
Till empires explode in ablutions
And we find a new savior to flay.

To pray is to get what we paid for
And death is the softest caress—
If evil is not what we're made for
Then why did He make us of flesh?

PART FOUR

From the Diary of Avram Parr

April 23, 2015

This entry will be brief. The fatal hour has nearly come. The excitement and trepidation radiating off me. The world, now that I am on the verge of exiting it, seems stiller, more supple, more charged with meaning.

Perhaps this is the key to freedom: to be willing to give up everything. If it all goes wrong, then it was meant to be that way. I am convinced of that now.

Whereas great men of the past were made great by their fame, great men of the future must exist in the shadows. Under democracy, to be exceptional is to be a threat. One is meant to exist only within the parameters of the hive mind.

But I have found an even more thorough solution: to cease to exist.

(17)

Mona might have told the voice on the phone that she had not in fact read any good poems lately, for she had been rather busy, but the line immediately went dead. A few moments later a text message appeared suggesting that she arrive at the grounds of the tech campus at eight o'clock that evening. It was signed—*Avram*.

Back in her apartment, Mona took out the hunter's knife—the same one she had borrowed from Del after Parr had broken into her home—and found that with some duct tape, she was able to secure it against the inside cloth of her hoodie. She didn't expect she would have cause to use it, but was not wholly averse to the thought of doing so, under the right circumstances. Her fingers trembled as she locked her door and proceeded out into the damp evening air.

The tech campus seemed even more grotesque this afternoon than it had on the dawn trip Mona made a few days prior. Like many developments paid for by the billion, it gave the sense of being not so much ahistorical as inimical to history, as though with these jagged glass windows and cement beams, the builders had meant to tear out past and future by the roots and replace them with a cold, anaesthetized, everlasting present. Flat-screen monitors had already been assembled and mounted in the empty lobbies, and bore messages such as CAMPUS SAFETY & SECURITY TIPS and FOLLOW US ONLINE. One monitor posed such queries as *What is Beauty?*, *What is*

Art?, *What is Innovation?*, and *What is Power?* Mona did not keep her eyes trained on it long enough to take in the proposed answers, except to see that the answer to *What is Innovation?* began: "Founded in 2010, Proserpina..."

"Pardon me," a voice behind Mona said, "but are you Mona Veigh, the distinguished poet? The one working on an epic about how the sky is blue?"

Mona turned to look at the man who had spoken. It was Parr and yet it was not Parr. Or rather, Mona realized, it was him in the same way a man can be himself in a dream, even when his face is someone else's. Whereas the Parr she had known had been gaunt to the point of skeletal, this new one was beefed up, and thick around the jowls. His once-thin lips were now full. His skin was bronzed, but not in a healthy-looking way. Only the icy green of his eyes remained unchanged.

"You look different," Mona said.

"I *am* different," Parr said, and his eyes appeared to flicker. "As a matter of fact, I feel like a whole new man."

He patted his face in mock-wonderment. Mona noticed that his middle and ring fingers were about two inches longer than they should have been.

"What have you done to yourself?"

"Ah, the fingers," Parr said, "an odd side effect, truly. The medical term for it is arachnodactyly. Do you like that word? When I first heard it I thought of you: I thought, this is a word Mona Veigh would like."

"For God's sake," Mona said.

Parr paused as if to make certain this was a negative reaction, and continued on.

"Walk with me," he said. "I have a place in mind where we can have a nice private little chat."

Parr touched his touch pass to a reader on one of the jagged building's glass doors, and they went past the monitor that offered the secrets of innovation and power, into a shining steel elevator bay. Ostentatiously, Parr used his long ring finger to press the button and summon their ride.

"It's a side effect of genomic engineering. CRISPR-X's viral replication process triggers mutations in fibrillin-1 and fibrillin-2 genes, which code for the length of one's fingers and toes. I don't have a firm understanding of it at the molecular level, but someone at CRISPR-X could break it down for us, surely. You should have seen Chris Rosecrans's index finger toward the end. It gained a good five inches. I took photographs."

"Before you chopped it off."

"It might have raised questions at the morgue. But once his gene-editing treatment was complete, he looked so much like me—or the old me, I should say—that I don't imagine anyone would have protested too much. In any case, his DNA sequences mirrored mine, and that's what people really care about. They want the hard data, yes? Numbers, sequences, alleles."

The elevator went down. Deep down, it seemed, beyond where a basement might reasonably be. Mona gripped the steel handle of her knife to steady her nerves: it was a comfort to know she had it. But the two of them merely stood there, still and silent and in the darkness. Mona resolved not to do anything rash. What was important was that he talked.

The elevator car finally stopped, and the doors opened to reveal a long cement corridor, lit by a row of evenly spaced hanging bulbs.

"I wanted to show you my workshop," Parr said. "CRISPR-X and Purusha have laboratories down here. But I suppose your friend at the NYPD has told you all that."

Mona felt herself go pale.

"I have eyes everywhere," Parr said. "You thought I didn't know you'd been in touch with the authorities about me? But it's all right, I don't mind. I trust you, Mona. Don't ask me why, but I do. Let me give you the tour."

"I don't want the tour. What I want is for you to explain some things to me."

"All right then," Parr said and shrugged his shoulders. "Your loss."

He led her through the first door on their left. Inside was a bare-bones office, with two metal chairs on either side of a collapsible table, and a whiteboard tacked to the plaster wall. Parr sat and motioned for her to do the same.

"This is the little room where I like to hold business meetings with some of my most trusted associates. Not much fear of being intruded upon. Fire away."

"Your people at CRISPR-X have found a way to exchange a person's DNA with someone else's, making each of them genetically unrecognizable. Something like that?"

"They're not the only ones who've figured it out," Parr said. "They're just the only ones who have been empowered to move forward with the available technology. I like for things to move quickly. Any other tough ones?"

He asked her this cheerfully, as though he were an elementary school teacher proud of a curious child.

"Yes. Why were you having me followed? What do *I* have to do with all this?"

"*That*," Parr said, "is an excellent question."

Parr got up from his seat and began to pace in excitement.

"It would actually be quite funny," he said, "if it were not so very sad. All the ordinary people in the world are gradually becoming convinced that they're extraordinary—that's what the marketing departments want them to believe, and the marketing departments are for the most part winning. Yet the extraordinary people like you often have no idea at all what they're worth."

"I created a program that allows a computer to write passably interesting poetry. I don't see what's so terribly extraordinary about that."

"Then you ought to step back for a moment and *look*. What do you think the world runs on, Mona? It doesn't run on algorithms or blood transfusions or even gene sequences, much as I might like it to. It runs on language, that funny little thing you specialize in. It runs on the stories we tell—whether they're true or false, intelligent or stupid—about what the world is and what it could be. About what *we* are and what *we* could be.

Now, some of the sillier and more small-minded stories—the ones we call morality, I mean—have lately become major stumbling blocks to me in my endeavors."

"You're trying to say that people don't like it when you kill people for your own selfish ends, yes?"

"Oh Mona," Parr said, "don't be so obtuse. I know you're not one of those resentful little people who can't see the larger picture. To be quite frank with you, it's my altruism that's to blame, if any of my actions ought to be considered blameworthy. My thoughts are of nothing but society and how it might flourish. Anti-aging technology, gene-editing procedures—these are new frontiers that will transform civilization as we know it. And they can do so not just centuries down the road, but today! Now if it so happens that overcautious bureaucrats with their red tape and their envy of people who actually *do* things mean to delay the use of these technologies for hundreds of years, can I really be faulted for taking things into my own hands?"

"And if all these gene-editing and blood-swapping technologies happen to lengthen and improve *your* own life, then I suppose this is just incidental."

"Honestly, Mona, you think I'd go through all this—extract myself from my company, my colleagues, from society at large—just for my own personal benefit? It's absurd. It would be a profoundly stupid strategy if my main goal were *happiness*—or whatever it is that most people live for. No, my mission is rather more ambitious. A new society, one ordered by reason, imagination, and the drive to move the species forward—that has been my aim for Proserpina from the beginning. It may be, however, that my vision for society is more... panoramic than usual. *I* can see, for instance, that life grows out of death, that there will always be a certain number of people who need to suffer so that a new world can be born. But this is only to say I'm less of a hypocrite than those pale criminals calling themselves government officials, who shed blood when it suits them and then wring their hands over it once the war is won."

"I see," Mona said, "so when most people commit atrocities, they feel a pang of conscience. But you're capable of fully justifying to yourself the murders you commit, so you can commit them guiltlessly. And therein lies your advantage over other moral actors. Am I getting this all right?"

Parr flashed her a crooked smile.

"The fact of the matter," he said, "is that we're all subject to terrible suffering no matter what. The only question to be answered is whether suffering should have a purpose. I say *yes*. The experts all agree that it would be a fine thing, were the population of the earth to drop by half. Yet none of them have the moral imagination to consider how such a remedy might be achieved. If four billion of the worst-off could die painlessly and at once, why would this not be preferable to their dying painfully after endless, humiliating toil—toil which only serves to enrich the profit share of the corporations to whom they're enslaved? Now imagine that this halving of the human population could usher us into a new age of unparalleled prosperity—into an age in which men and women indeed become as gods and goddesses. Would it not be worth it? Would it not in fact be our moral obligation to bring such an event to be?"

Parr was now speaking so rapidly that the words seemed to usher forth from him without conscious thought. It was no longer a conversation, but a continuously flowing stream of sound. Mona ran her hand over the knife in her sweatshirt.

"Soon these questions will no longer be hypothetical. The technologies being developed at Purushsa and CRISPR-X have the power to bring forth a species greater than the merely human, a species of hominids that could live for centuries at a time and remedy their own genetic deficiencies on their own. And yet it is only with the aid of Hildegard 2.0 that all of this moves into the realm of reality."

"*2.0?*" Mona said. A sick feeling arose in her stomach.

"It's an idea I've been developing since soon after I met you," Parr chirped, "really, it's frighteningly simple. You fed Hildegard lines of poetry, and it learned how to write its own poems—poems, as you've told me many times, that have a real sense of individuality. Well, I'll feed Hildegard 2.0 all kinds of data, and it will learn to tell an individualized story—whatever story that person most wants to hear. Think about it! What, for instance, would the perfect Mona-story be? Some intellectual hijinks, some moving poetry, some spleen, some satire, a good deal of mystery at the vast strangeness of the universe, and perhaps even the possibility of redemption, to top things off. What do you think? Sounds like a reality you might like to inhabit, no? You know, when I brought our first social media start-up into the fold a decade ago, it was because I intuited that these technologies do not actually *connect* us all at all. What they do is show us the versions of the world—the pictures, the stories—that their algorithms have learned we most want to see. They put us all in our own bubbles. And people *love* living in bubbles. It makes the world so much less complicated. Hildegard 2.0, then, will be social media's final frontier. It will tell people the stories they most want to hear, with a little bit of what's good for them thrown in here and there. It's social media without all the pesky and painful incursions of opinions and arguments which are not in perfect agreement with the user's own tastes—and at this point we can deduce our users' tastes before they know them themselves. Hildegard 2.0 will be personal shopper, therapist, and guru all rolled into one!"

After seeming to exhaust his capacity for wild pacing, Parr turned to Mona and paused.

He scanned her face for a sign.

"You don't seem to be excited by the transformative potential of Hildegard 2.0."

"You want to turn my work into a personalized propaganda machine that you'll use to convince people of the necessity of eugenics, and you're asking if I'm excited."

"Propaganda! Propaganda, she says. What a miserable word. It conjures the notion of a hot-blooded American at a podium somewhere, shouting 'Better Dead than Red.' A most unfortunate thought. I have to admit, actually, I admire the Soviets. At least they had the ambition to try to improve human nature. At least they had an ideal! But no, Mona, propaganda is not what we're talking about here. We're talking about a revolution in consciousness—algorithmically enhanced minds, algorithmically enhanced life! Here, I want to show you something. Would you kindly follow me, please?"

Parr exited the makeshift conference room without waiting for an answer. For the greater part of his speech Mona had felt frozen to her chair as though under a spell. But she had awakened from it once Hildegard was brought up, and it dawned on her that her own work, her own ideals, had been integrated into the madness of what she was now confronting. She reminded herself that she had a weapon, to be used as needed.

"Are you aware that this used to be a prison site?" Parr asked.

"I've read the Roosevelt Island guidebook, yes. And the building I live in used to be an asylum. But I suppose you know that already, since you've spent so much time shadowing my movements."

"As a matter of fact I did know it," Parr said. He pulled an old-fashioned metal key from his pocket and inserted it into a hole in the wall, which might easily have been mistaken for a blotch of dirt. A rectangular portion of the wall slowly creaked open. Beyond this hidden door was darkness. Parr stepped into the room and began:

"The penitentiary and the madhouse—the two poles of our civilization."

He found the switch and flipped it. A single bulb crackled on and illuminated the room with faint yellow light. Mona first spotted a metal desk in the corner: it reminded her eerily of the one in her own room. Then she saw a toilet bowl jutting out from the opposite wall and a dirty cot beside it.

"The penitentiary or the madhouse—those are the two places to which you are liable to be banished if you do not heed the call of the herd. Right now we're in the penitentiary. What do you think? I've had it lovingly preserved. Once upon a time it was an underground cell reserved for Roosevelt Island's most dangerous prisoners. I have it on good authority that they constructed it for Dutch Harmon, the notorious highwayman, after he escaped with seven other prisoners shackled to him by ball and chain. But they never did find Dutch, so they must have brought some equally deserving criminal here in his stead. Look! I even managed to have this charming artifact brought back to life."

Parr went to the desk and pulled out what was evidently a cattle prod.

"It took weeks to find a battery compatible with such an outdated item. But now it's as good as new."

He pressed a button, and the weapon buzzed and glowed menacingly. "Why are you showing me this?" Mona asked.

"Only as a helpful illustration," Parr said, "of the prison side of things. This is the sort of place the state would like to put me, if they thought I was still alive. All these cops and judges and histrionic moralists—they could never stand to see me truly free. And not just because of the experiments I performed at Purusha. But as a matter of principle. The mere existence of someone like me is enough to send them and the mob that backs them into a rage. It's a fact, you know—a fact so obvious that no one dares discuss it—that there exists a vast disparity in intelligence and other forms of evolutionary fitness between the highest functioning members of the species and the median. And good God does this inspire the median with a desire for vengeance, if they get to thinking about it too much. Maybe you don't like to hear this sort of thing spoken out loud more than anyone else does. Maybe it makes you feel guilty. You see, that's your characteristic danger, on the other side of the spectrum from mine: you believe them when they tell you there's something wrong with you, simply because you don't take pleasure in what they do. Then you let it *eat* at you. That's how you ended up on the side of madness, Mona. You decided you didn't *want* to be part of the ad-clicking, Candy Crush-playing horde, but when you escaped there was no one there to meet you on the other side. You may think that I have no human discernment, but I've been watching you carefully since the day we met. I know you—perhaps better than you know yourself."

"Quite the speech," Mona said, "and is *that* why you and your underlings have been following me around all this time? To fill out a psychological portrait?"

"It was rather a fringe benefit," Parr said, and gave an embarrassed smile, "but the fact is that my team of developers is quite small since I went underground, and we need the code for Hildegard. That QR code scavenger hunt you set up really has been quite an amusing diversion. But for the last week or so we've been trying in vain to get to the last one, and I must say I'm beginning to get rather frustrated. You wouldn't happen to know where it's hidden, would you?"

Mona's stomach dropped. She hadn't been monitoring her email for new poems from Hildegard and did not know just how many of the codes had been scanned. All this time she had been ignoring her creation as it unfurled its own story in verse. Yet while she was dismayed, Mona could not help but smile. So that's what this is all about, she thought, the code. He needs the ones and the zeros, nothing more. She remembered the Swinburne poem in the *Norton Anthology*, next to which she had placed the final QR code necessary to access Hildegard. The last place Parr and his henchmen would have ever deigned to look—inside of a book.

"Now it's up for you to choose," Parr said, "do you want to join me and be part of the future, part of something truly great? Or do you want to go back to your madhouse, loving what others treat with indifference, silently smoldering with hatred?"

"I suppose if I were to choose the first option, what you have in mind is my faking my own death and disappearing into your underground world."

"That would certainly be ideal. I could use someone of your caliber. But either way, I need that code. And within the next forty-eight hours. I'll give you the encrypted address where you can send it to me."

"And if I don't?"

"I do have my ways," Parr said, "of getting what I want." He flipped the switch of the cattle prod in his hand and held it up above his head, marveling at it as though it were the first flame Prometheus had brought down to mortals. "It's truly amazing," he continued, "how much creative energy is freed up once one begins to value one's desires ahead of conventional morality. It occurs to me to observe, for instance, just how far we are beneath the ground, just how futile any terrible shrieks you might emit would be—that is, if something unforeseen, something truly awful were to happen to you."

Mona pulled the knife out from its hold at her hip and pointed it at Parr. Her grip was firm. She was prepared to do whatever she might have to do.

"If two people attack each other underground," she said, "and there's no one there to hear them scream, has anyone even been killed?"

Parr smiled. "Ah, but how silly we are," he said, "to be speculating about such things. We may both be criminals at heart—and I do believe we are—but I'm certain neither of us are brutes. And that is a crucial distinction. Here, let me walk you back to the elevator. It's like a labyrinth down here. Fortunate that you have me as a guide—otherwise it might be very easy to lose one's way."

"You first," Mona said. "I'll have you where I can see you."

Parr flipped off the light for the prison cell and walked out into the corridor, making confident strides back toward the entrance.

"Really," he said, in the voice he used when attempting to approximate humor, "you mustn't be paranoid."

Mona kept the knife gripped firmly in her hand as they walked. Halfway to the elevator Parr stopped and turned to her.

"But I do want to be serious for a moment," he said. "The world that you've made your home in is dying. I mean poetry, and that sort of humanistic tripe. I want you to be aware of that. You're talented, and the skills that you've developed will be incredibly useful for the new world that's going to be built over the next quarter- or half-century. But make no mistake, there's a breach that's about to open up. The gulf will widen between those who tell stories, and those who believe them—who let their lives be run by and consumed by them. So you'll have to decide, Mona, do you really think there's magic in your precious poetry? Do you think so even when you can write the code to produce that supposed magic? Are you going to be the enchanter or the enchanted? Could you really be so credulous as to believe your own fairy tales?"

Mona only stared at him. She put the knife back in its hold. "Let's walk," she said.

And she followed him back to the elevator and up toward the light. But when she emerged back above ground the sky was dark and angry, and a heavy rain had begun to fall.

(18)

The next day Mona called Aldo to update him, and to give him the details of the plan she had come up with.

"I'm working from home today," he said, "why don't you drop by early this evening, and we'll talk. We wouldn't want you to do anything rash."

"This is my business now," Mona said, "I'll do exactly as I please."

"Mona," Aldo said, "that's been plenty clear from the beginning. But come over anyhow. I'm making turkey pot pie, and let me tell you something since you've never had my homemade turkey pot pie before: this isn't the sort of thing you want to miss. Say 5:30?"

Aldo's house was on the bottom floor of a white clapboard duplex on a street lined with dozens of other white clapboard duplexes. Mrs. Aldo greeted Mona at the door. She had kind, sad eyes and wore a thick knit sweater. Mona hardly knew what to say to her or to the children, who seemed to like her—although she gave them no encouragement.

"This isn't my strong suit," she said as they sat down around the dinner table. She didn't specify whether she meant small talk, or being around kids, or even perhaps the act of using a fork and knife to consume food at a table in the evening time. But Mrs. Aldo smiled with muted understanding.

"Batman," said eight-year-old Johnny, "wears a strong suit. It's made of adamantium."

"I'm Peppa Pig," said six-year-old Francesca, "oink oink oink oink."

"Eat your salad greens," Mrs. Aldo said.

"Oink oink oink," Francesca said, "oink oink oink oink."

"I'm not sure I would care for that," Mona said to Aldo once they'd retired to his study, "the oinking."

Aldo laughed. "You get used to it. Mind if I light a cigar?"

"Go for it."

Aldo extracted himself from his easy chair and went to crack a window. The room was lit dimly by a floor lamp. Aldo sat back down and slowly, lovingly ran the flame of his lighter over the far end of the cigar, taking little puffs to get it fired throughout.

"I don't want you to go out there," he said. "Just send Parr the code and we'll track him. We'll find him somehow."

"You won't even be able to convince your people that he's alive."

"He'll slip up," Aldo said.

"He won't."

The cigar's ripe, musky smell filled the room. Mona looked through smoke into Aldo's eyes: under the heavy lids she saw something both preoccupied and plaintive. He was looking just to the side of Mona, grimacing slightly, breathing heavily in between puffs. By now Mona had learned that if Aldo was not talking a mile a minute, something was wrong. She could not understand yet what it was, why he was against the plan she had proposed over the phone, which obviously was their best opportunity to bring Parr to justice. But a familiar feeling rose within her, and she knew intuitively, if not rationally, that this feeling held the answer. It was that sensation of overpowering sympathy to which she was sometimes prone, and which had absorbed her for a brief period during her first meeting with Aldo.

"I'm telling you, Mona," he said, "just give him the code. You'll be out of this mess, and meanwhile I'll be working day and night to bring him out into the open and get the law on board with me."

Mona watched the lines of his wide, fleshy face shift as he grimaced and took another puff of his cigar. She could tell that her own silence affected him: he had been expecting a barrage of arguments, but instead Mona simply held eye contact and waited.

Aldo blurted out, "I don't want to see you hurt, Mona. I wouldn't be able to live with myself."

A great relief came over Mona, for this was clearly the first sincere thing that had been said since their conversation began. Mona noticed the sensation of sympathy surge within her. But just before it did so she was able to match it with its cause. Namely, an event was taking place that had occurred only rarely before in her life—someone was showing genuine concern for her. Aldo's concern, she knew, was not because she was a great programmer or a scholar, or because she was of use to him in any way. It was simply for her as a soul that existed. The feeling welled up inside her and she found herself doing a very strange thing: she walked over to him through the pungent smoke and put her hand on his shoulder.

"Why do you care?" she said.

Aldo smiled. "For the same reason," he said, "that I put up with oinking at the dinner table."

"Because you want an heir to carry on the family name? I'm flattered, but—"

"No, I'm afraid it isn't that. It's that at a certain point you realize you've got a role to play in life. It doesn't have so much to do with what you like or what you don't like, Mona. It has to do with what's real and what's not real, and making a priority out of the real. I'm hoping that makes sense—it's one of those things that's easier to live out than it is to explain, if you follow me."

And on this rare instance, Mona did follow him. The redness around her eyes was evidence enough.

"It's just from the smoke," she said.

"Of course it is," Aldo said, and neither of them felt they had to say any more.

*

Back at her own home Mona took out her cherished *Norton Anthology* and turned to the page with the fateful QR code affixed to it. "Hildegard," she whispered, as though trying to summon up her patron saint to get advice about how she ought to proceed. Parr had begged her to allow him to change the name when he bought the company. "You can keep it something poetry-related," he had said, "how about *Lord Byron*? I've heard of that one, and people seem to be intrigued by him. His name has the word *lord* in it."

But Mona insisted that she keep the name. Hildegard of Bingen, aka Saint Hildegard, was a hero to Mona. This twelfth-century woman was a nun, a poet, a musician, a mystic, and, when she had a little spare time, the first practitioner of modern biology in Europe. *Polymath* was an understatement. And beyond all her officially recognized accomplishments, Hildegard had a more mysterious notch in her belt. Namely, something she called Lingua Ignota, or, "the unknown language."

Lingua Ignota used an alphabet of twenty-three letters to form words that looked like a mélange of German and Latin. And Hildegard created a glossary of Lingua Ignota words for all the most important concepts known to the people in her set—from *man* to *woman* to *virgin* to *God*. (She did not neglect, however, to create words for such lovable minor players in the world drama as *ankle*, *cornflower*, and *duck*.) Hildegard wedged this glossary for her invented language between theological manuscripts without comment; she never did write down what it was *for*, nor was there evidence that she ever showed it to another soul. Some modern commentators— blinded, Mona believed, by their overly rationalistic outlook—contended that the Lingua was an early attempt at something like Esperanto, that is, a universal language that might facilitate conversation between diverse groups. Mona strongly disagreed. She had studied Lingua Ignota and had even read a few of Hildegard's theological treatises. But her opinion was not based on this study. It was intuitive, and yet it was as certain as anything she had ever come to know through research or logical induction. Mona's opinion was this: Hildegard had meant for her invented language to be completely private—it had been a means of separating language from its coarser function as mere communication. Language, Mona knew, and knew that Hildegard knew, was not just sense but also sound. A spell could be woven from the proper string of phonemes, just as magic could be summoned by a correctly performed dance or an enchanted amulet. Hildegard had meant to slough off all that was menial and mundane in language: her Lingua Ignota was a way for her to form her prayers with greater verve and purity, to speak not to others but to the part of herself that was most numinous and true, and which she called, following tradition, *God*.

And as Mona sat staring at this page of the anthology in her quiet apartment, turning over in her mind the possibilities of the next few days, Mona felt within herself a kinship with Hildegard, a sense that she too had been inventing her own private language, and using it to ascertain something ineffable. Hildegard the program had indeed functioned for her as a divining rod, though it was never entirely clear what the program meant for Mona to divine. It had something to do, she could say, with the intermingling of technology and language: of brute computation and ineffable spirit. Mona made herself a cup of coffee and looked out her high window at the lights of the city beyond and contemplated different versions of the future. She saw herself carrying out the plan she had suggested to Aldo, or, alternately, joining Parr in his underground technocratic coup, or simply disappearing from New York and trying to start all over again. And only now did it occur to her *exactly* why the program she had created felt so utterly separate from what Parr and his colleagues saw in it—and what made Mona herself feel separate, at that. Although Hildegard and other projects like it were called intelligent machines, Mona felt that its intelligence ultimately proceeded from some other place. She saw it as more like a clump of tea leaves or the I Ching, that ancient Chinese fortune-telling text, than as a typical scientific tool. She could explain the logic behind the algorithm she had created, just as she could explain the social forces behind the work of any favorite poet. But the poems themselves she could not fully explain.

There was something in them that was irreducible. In the silence of her apartment Mona took a moment to try to sense what it was, this irreducible *thing* beneath Hildegard's poems, and beneath her own life. As she pondered this, a euphoric feeling came over her. Her familiar studio seemed to radiate energy, as when, on certain rainy April days, the sky clears and the world suddenly shifts from one season to the next, and the wind is wild, and the contours of the known universe seem to be suffused with an uncontainable magnetic charge. On days like that and indeed this evening it could feel as though what we all accept as reality is only a symptom of some mysterious underlying cause. Years ago Mona had read the work of a historian who suggested that the transformations of ideas (and thus of life itself) across centuries might follow some yet unknown mathematical principle. The historian had thought he had found a clue in fractals, those long sequences of numbers that form beautiful, enigmatic spirals when plotted on a graph. No one had discovered fractals until computers were invented: to deduce their pattern required so many iterations that it would have been impossible to find the pattern by hand. But once the pattern was discovered, people noticed that fractals appeared everywhere in nature—from pinecones to weather patterns to the seemingly (though not actually) random intervals at which drops of water from a leaky faucet fall.

And if in nature and in numbers, then why not in poetry, why not in life? It could be that technology really was putting humans in place to witness a leap forward—but not the sort of leap forward the techno-optimists imagined. It was not that our achievements in the realm of ones and zeroes would allow us to turn the world into heaven on earth. Rather it was that they helped us discern the heaven that had always been there, and the hell too, swirling above and below the median level existence of which we were conscious. And as Mona turned over this thought in her mind, it seemed to her that fate had already foreordained her next move, and she knew exactly what to do.

(19)

That night Mona texted Parr to tell him she would give him the code he so desired and go with him underground. But she wanted to give it in person, so couldn't they meet up again, and somewhere other than his subterranean lair. It wasn't the sort of place one looks forward to returning to, she said. Parr countered with Lighthouse Park, an empty expanse ten minutes by foot from the Octagon, on the very northern end of Roosevelt Island. Mona suspected that the tunnel system extended all the way there from the tech campus, and that Parr wanted to stay near an entrance to it in case any part of their transaction went awry. She drew in a deep breath and agreed.

On the appointed evening Mona put the Norton's Anthology and a recently purchased walkie-talkie into her big hoodie pocket. She left the Octagon two hours early to search for underground passages, along with any other potential obstacles. The park was entirely empty. A row of willows rustled overhead in the wind and the rain. Streetlamps, placed about ten feet apart from one another, dotted the outer rim of the island on both shorelines. Mona walked down the west side first, looking for openings into the earth. From where would Parr emerge? She kept her head down, watching the contours of her shadow shift as she moved in and out of the scattered light. An abrupt shrill noise startled her—but Mona looked up to find it was only a gaggle of ducks, their plump little bodies wobbling as they flew out over the river and into the mist.

Mona continued on to the very northern tip of the island, where a disused lighthouse, twenty feet high, stood at the promontory's center. Mona thought of ships from years past that must have sailed by its light, in a world that had not yet been made exhaustively navigable. She made an about-face here and walked back in the opposite direction along the island's eastern edge. Into and out of the light of the streetlamps, she and her shadow made their way. There did not appear to be any entrances to the underground on this side of the riverwalk either. Nor were there any holes in the earth along the grassy expanse that lay between the two shorelines. Mona found herself now at the end of the park farthest from the lighthouse, within shouting distance of a parking lot where two police cars loitered. She gave one of the cars a wave but was not quite close enough to see if anyone inside waved back.

Presently Mona turned from the parking lot and saw two distant figures walking toward her, from the very end of the island. But where had they come from? There was no road there, and Mona had been watching the footpaths carefully to make sure nobody passed her on either side. The figures walked slowly, in lockstep. Mona recognized Parr first. It was difficult to mistake his mincing gait: it was as though he were stepping with bare feet over glass. The other man was taller and bulkier, and once he stepped directly under a streetlamp, Mona saw that it was Marcos. Anxiety took hold of her as she thought over the fact that they seemed to have appeared miraculously out of the fog. But she calmed herself and determined to think quickly. She saw Marcos wave as he approached, holding his arm stiff in the air. Parr made his delicate steps forward, looking at nothing in particular.

It was only once they were face-to-face with her, as the wind picked up and stirred the leaves of the willows into a frenzy, that it occurred to her: the lighthouse. To Mona's knowledge it had not been put to its official use for years. But it still had a door, and perhaps, for some unknown nautical reason, it had a basement level. If so, Parr could have found a way to connect it with his underground labyrinth.

"I didn't know we were supposed to bring our seconds to this duel," Mona said to Parr, "but it's all right. I don't think I could have found anyone, anyway."

"Sorry we didn't get to talk things over much," Marcos said. "I've been busy."

"That's what all the boys say."

"I'm going to assume," Parr said, "that this is a kind of flirtatious joking, which is being used to offset the tenseness of the situation. However, I am eager to receive the code Mona has promised and prefer that we hasten on to that stage of the interaction."

"Yes, I'm doing very well this evening, thank you," Mona said, "and yourself? Oh yes, I agree, it *was* very kind of me to come out here and bring you the code, given all that I've been through."

"You could have just sent it to me like a normal person. There is such a thing as encryption. But you always *were* paranoid."

"Which didn't mean they weren't after me, it turned out."

"Hand over the flash drive, please," Parr said.

"Flash drive?" Mona said. "What makes you think I've brought a flash drive?"

"I don't follow," Parr said.

"Oh, I brought you something much more interesting, instead!" Mona took the anthology out from her backpack.

"A book," Marcos said.

"I always liked that about you," Mona said, "how observant you are." She opened it up to Swinburne's "Hymn to Proserpine" and read:

> For the glass of the years is brittle wherein we gaze for a span;
> A little soul for a little bears up this corpse which is man.
> So long I endure, no longer; and laugh not again, neither weep.
> For there is no God found stronger than death; and death is a sleep.

"It jingle-jangles," Parr said, "but it does not appear to mean much."

"It means that all this is coming to an end," Mona said.

"All what is?" Marcos said.

"Our time together, for one thing," Mona said.

"I am hoping desperately," Parr said, "that this all leads somehow to your handing over to me the code."

"Oh. That," Mona said. "Yes, as a matter of fact."

She turned the book around so that the pages faced him and cracked open the spine. Parr spotted the QR code.

"A flair for the dramatic," he said, "are you expecting me to scan that now with my phone?"

"No, you can just have it," Mona said. She slammed the book shut. "But first you'll have to take it from me."

No one spoke in response to this. Mona held the book above her head, like a school bully taunting a smaller child.

"I'm afraid I don't understand," Parr said.

"You're supposed to be a genius," Mona said, "it's not so difficult. Take the book from me and you can have it."

Parr and Marcos exchanged glances. Mona saw Marcos form his large, hairy hands into fists.

"But no help from your goon," she said, "this code contains only half of what you'll need to access Hildegard. If you can get the book from me fair and square, Parr, I'll happily supply the supplementary material. But if Marcos steps in, no dice."

This was a lie, but she could tell immediately from Parr's frozen stare that he believed it.

Mona realized that she had got rather good by now at off-the-cuff deception.

"Now I want a good clean fight. No biting. No scratching. And nothing below the belt—the last of which is a very gentlewomanly concession, on my part."

"This is absurd," Parr said, "and it is beneath you, for that matter."

"Or is it simply," Mona said, "that no one ever taught you how to fight? Come on, I thought you were some kind of overman, who's going to set the world to rights. But you can't even get up the gumption to fight little old me?"

Parr's eyes betrayed equal amounts of confusion and rage, although he had worked his mouth up into the twisted approximation of a smile.

"And I'll tell you why," she continued, "because you're no great thinker, you're no great visionary, you're nothing. All those grand words about prisons and madhouses are just a cover for the fact that you're a grasping little weakling, you've always been a grasping little weakling, and now you want your revenge against the world. Well, take it! Take it from me then!"

Parr lunged at her, one hand making for the book, the other for her throat. But Mona took a step to the side, using his forward motion against him to toss him to the ground. He leapt up immediately and attempted to seize her by the waist.

But Mona slipped away from his grasp. She grabbed the walkie-talkie from her hoodie pocket. "Now!" Mona shouted into the device, "now! And have someone cover the lighthouse, that's where they came in from!"

"Who is she talking to?" Marcos said, "shit, shit, shit."

From the parking lot with the idling police car Aldo appeared. He marched toward them, his gun in hand and directed at Parr.

"Step away from her," he bellowed, "and put your hands above your head."

Parr, like a surprised child who has been caught out in his mischief, froze and then took a few steps backward, hands in the air.

"What seems to be the problem?" he said.

"Keep your hands where I can see them," Aldo said, "and you too," he barked at Marcos.

Marcos lifted his arms slowly and mechanically—nearly the same movement he had made when he'd waved.

"You didn't tell me there'd be two of them," Aldo said to Mona.

"I didn't know. They came up out of the ground from the lighthouse. Have your men cover it."

"Roger that," Aldo said. With his free hand he took his own walkie-talkie from his belt and relayed Mona's instructions.

"I didn't expect this from you," Parr said, still grinning, "you've impressed me."

"Save it," Aldo said.

"I'm sorry officer, but have I committed a crime?" Parr said.

"Many," Aldo said, "but the one I get to take you in on is assault, which I happen to have just witnessed. So you can just stay right where you are, and in a minute I'll have some friends of mine help you into a squad car."

"But me?" Marcos said, "I'm innocent."

"Innocent as Judas Iscariot himself," Aldo said. "False papers, false badge, false smile, false everything—and we haven't even got started with what we might call your. . . reckless driving back down in Oklahoma. So you can just hold tight."

"I can't fault you for this, Mona." Parr said. "After all, it would be rather inconsistent of me. I've always believed that in any battle the spoils ought to go to the cleverest party."

As he spoke he lowered his hands down from directly above his head to the level of his chest, palms upward in a sign of what appeared to be supplication.

"Hands up!" Aldo said and turned his gun toward Parr. "Up in the air, now!"

But Parr left his hands where they were and took a step toward Aldo. He exchanged glances with Marcos, and a strangely serene expression appeared on his face.

"How could I possibly judge, after all? People pretend as though they can say which actions are right or wrong, good or bad—but they can't. Just as there are a million shades of light we can't see, but we go on calling the grass green, or the sky blue, or what have you. . . well, there are a million shades of right and wrong that most people insist on labeling either good or bad. But I won't bother with that."

"Don't take another step," Aldo said, "or I'll shoot!"

But Parr took another step, and another.

"I suppose," Parr said, "my misfortune is that I can see shades other people can't." He took another step forward. Aldo tensed his finger against the trigger.

"Who knows, after all, how we'll be judged in the future? The future is like a color that doesn't exist."

Out of the corner of her eye Mona saw Marcos move his hand into his pocket and pull out his own gun. She threw herself at him and shouted out to warn Aldo.

What came next was pure confusion: it all happened so quickly that Mona could not take in the events as discrete occurrences. When she thought back on it later, the chronology all seemed squished together, as in one of those devotional paintings where Christ's birth and the performance of miracles and death are all depicting in adjoining panels. The first thing Mona noticed was the gunshot: it would have been impossible to miss. But she could not tell from where it had issued or where it had struck. Then she saw Parr grab the book from her and run. That was what lodged itself most vividly in her mind, it was so incongruous. Parr did not seem the type to run—Mona wouldn't have guessed that his body was even capable of it. And yet there he was, sprinting toward the lighthouse, his shadow waxing and waning as he passed under successive streetlamps.

Then came the sirens. Mona heard them before she saw the flashing red and blue lights they accompanied. And then the growl of tires as the police cars descended from the parking lot and cut across the grassy expanse. They raced past her toward the lighthouse: she had not realized cars could drive so well on lawn. She watched as one of the cars chased down Marcos, who was also running, but who had tripped and was immediately cuffed by two burly officers emerging from a car. And it was only then that Mona turned to see Aldo on the ground, just perceptibly twitching, lying in a shallow pool of his own blood. As though in a trance, she stepped toward him.

"God save us all," he said.

"Help!" Mona shouted, "somebody help this man!" But she could not be heard over the sirens.

"Help!" Mona shouted again.

"God save us," Aldo said faintly.

In the distance Mona saw Parr escape through the door of the lighthouse and latch it shut. Two officers close behind him banged on it and eventually resorted to shooting the lock.

"May my prayers be answered, may the Lord hear. God save us."

Mona pulled his shirt up a found the wound—a black and red craggy gash in his left side. Blood emptied from it and streamed slowly over the grass. Mona pulled off her hoodie and tried to tie it across the wound. But still she saw blood trickle down.

"May what has been foreordained come to pass. May the Lord forgive us our sins and have mercy on us all. God save us."

"You don't need God, you need a medic," Mona said. "Help!" she shrieked, "help!"

A new siren sounded. She saw an ambulance arrive at the parking lot and she waved her arms. A man emerged from it and rushed toward them. Mona knelt down and pressed her hand against his chest. She heard his heart beat strangely, desperately.

At that moment she would have given up everything she had ever had, every pleasure and every success, every moment of happiness past and future, that this suffering man should not perish. The footsteps of the medic came closer, and a last dram of blood oozed from Aldo's side. The sirens continued to ring out, and Aldo lifted his head to look directly into Mona's eyes.

"God save us," he said, and died.

(20)

That night the last thunderstorm of the season passed over the city; by morning it had become brilliantly sunny and warm. Pools of rainwater gathered in the divots along Roosevelt Island's badly paved Main Road, reflecting back the season's last tawny autumn leaves against a sheet of pale sky. Mona circled the island a dozen times that day. No stranger passing by would have guessed that anything was amiss with her. She walked with her head up, shoulders back, around and around the looping road. At dusk she stopped at the head of the island, looking out toward Lighthouse Park and the dark water beyond. The river beckoned to her, and for a moment she could imagine herself diving into it. She could feel the water enveloping her consciousness, leading her on toward the deepest dark sleep. But the moment passed. She had a reason now—more of a feeling, really, a sense of herself as part of a story that was only just beginning—to carry on.

 Aldo's funeral, a few days later, was tasteful and well-attended: a place in the family lot had been reserved for him at Calvary Cemetery in Queens. His wife shook Mona's hand, offered a brave smile, and thanked her for coming. His two small children scowled and shuffled their feet. His aged mother cried pitifully, and as soon as the corpse had been lowered, two large men took hold of her by each arm and escorted her back to the rusted mauve family minivan. (Aldo's father had been dead already for decades.) The low autumn sun shone mockingly on them as they listened to the priest's homily. Mona did not stay for the reception.

She bought a new laptop and used it regularly. Daylight saving came, and shortened her hours. Mostly they were now spent being interviewed by the authorities. A few of these men seemed to believe her when she told the truth about Parr. But the majority of them evidently thought she was batty, and it appeared that they had thought the same of Aldo. From certain asides and innuendo she gathered that many within the force had doubted Aldo's judgment even before his adventures with Mona had begun. They chalked his folly up to an excessive moral purity and a morbid imagination—both of which, it appeared to be the consensus, are apt to lead officers astray.

Marcos, who was being held without bail at Rikers Island, only a short boat ride from Roosevelt, gave them a story more plausible than Mona's, and stuck to it. To wit: that he had come to Lighthouse Park with his business associate, one Christian Rosecrans, in order to exchange certain sensitive documents they had acquired for a large sum of cash. That Mona, a confirmed paranoiac, had inveigled Detective Aldo into believing her bizarre delusion about Avram Parr's return from the dead. And that when Marcos saw a cop arrive on the scene that evening at the park, he had shot on impulse, to avoid being taken in for his many previous violent crimes. Rosecrans, whom Marcos claimed to have met years ago at a grow operation in California, was now on the lam—Marcos told the police he would do whatever he could to help locate him, but Rosecrans was a shady, slippery fellow, and if he were them he wouldn't hold his breath.

As for the lighthouse, the police informed Mona that it was indeed connected to the tech campus's underground network. But there was nothing so odd about this: it was to be converted early next year to a transmissions tower and integrated with the rest of the campus. Of course none of the construction workers had seen anyone resembling Avram Parr in the area. The officers who interviewed her made it clear that the very idea was absurd.

Mona could tell that a few of them suspected that she was responsible for Aldo's death. She didn't try especially hard to disabuse them of the idea. She just told them the truth, in the fewest number of words she could manage. She wasn't much concerned with what they thought. Her mind was elsewhere.

During one of these sessions, while Mona was looking out the window at the toggling red and green reflections of a stoplight, a particularly ill-natured investigator asked her:

"Do you even care that a good man is dead?"

"I do."

"Well it doesn't much show. How *would* you describe your current state of mind?"

"It isn't the sort of thing one much cares to describe."

The officer narrowed his eyes at her.

"And what are you going to do with yourself," he asked, "now that your adventures with the criminal underworld appear to be over?"

She wandered the city, as had long been her habit. But without anxiety or restlessness. The knowledge that she had come so close to the heart of things allayed all fear. Good and evil had touched her and now would be part of her. They could be summoned now on any bitter evening, as the wind hissed through the trees, and their shadows flickered across her windowpane. But fear would no longer stalk her through daylight.

Even something of Mona's physiology appeared to have changed. She now slept less, and yet felt less tired. Her vision now seemed clearer, while her flight of imaginative fancy had been tamped down. All in all the world seemed to her weightier and more real. No longer did she fret over the meaning behind unexplained sounds, odd coincidences, twilight apparitions. These were only expressions of inward evils, and she made her peace with them.

With Aldo's death something had been taken from her, and from that loss she gained new life. She took to reading mythical and religious tales: of Bahram Gur who consulted the Seven Beauties and restored justice to his land; of Iseult of the White Hands, who had no time for wild romance; of King Indra in the Puranas, who loved the world all the more after renouncing it; of the prodigal son returned. Shadows crept toward the water's edge as she read in afternoon light on a bench by the river, a few paces from her home. As night came, the lamplight would click on and set the undersides of autumn leaves aglow in lurid red and yellow. Roosevelt Island no longer felt like a safe haven to Mona, nor did the rest of the world feel like a threat. Though she remained alone for now, she no longer felt alienated from all those who passed before her. She no longer raged a technology's ever-increasing grip on the world: its annihilating tendency was inevitable and would just have to be accepted—at least until it had destroyed culture entirely, and something new could be built from the ruins. She no longer raised her fist against the tawdriness of the world, or felt worry rise through her body like a wave about to break, or shivered madly as she lay down to sleep. She no longer read poetry.

Except, that is, for a poem she received from an unknown sender, one bright morning just after the winter frost had set in. Mona sat with it in her condo for several days. It was a "Skeltonic," after an early English bard, loosely iambic and loosely rhyming. In its content it resembled the riddle poems of Taliesin and the kennings of Nordic skalds. Yet what it reminded Mona most of—and not for any strictly logical reason—was her old favorite, the poem that began with the lines "Stop All the Clocks." In that nearly one-hundred-year-old poem what had looked like tragedy had turned out to be comedy. In this poem that Mona received what looked like finality might, she thought, turn out merely to be beginning. Perhaps, she mused, this was an eccentric reading of the text. On the other hand, Mona felt she had an insight into the author's mind that no one else had. And in the poetic history of the world, there is always room for interpretation.

The subject line of the message containing the poem was "From an old and new friend." The message read:

Well Mona, here we are. Everything has a way of working itself out in the end, does it not? I certainly wish we could have parted on better terms, but, as I said once before, I simply cannot be angry with you. It just wouldn't do. Especially not since things have been moving along so splendidly for me since we last met. CRISPR-X has made some amazing advances just over the course of the last month, and it is now simpler than ever to make edits to one's appearance and gene composition on the fly. Purusha is showing greater signs of life each day. And Hildegard—well, Hildegard has simply been a joy. It will be rather simple to convert it to a program that produces reliable prose, in addition to poetry. (I want you to know that the prototype for the social media platform Hildegard will be used for has been code-named "Mona," in your honor.) But now I've only been playing around with iterating different poems. Which brings me to the main purpose of this missive. Yesterday Hildegard 2.0 produced a poem I felt I simply had to share with you. Be warned, it's rather a long one. I've been tweaking the code to get Hildegard 2.0 to produce longer and longer works. Eventually, I think, the program will center around prose narrative, as that seems to me the language-based medium which is most widely effective in entrancing the masses. Can you imagine? Each future user of Hildegard 2.0 will get a full-length narrative work dramatizing their deepest desires and fears, based on the information they've supplied to the program. I suppose eventually I should work in a module so that the user can choose his or her own ending.

 Back to the poem: I do not claim to know what it means, nor do I claim to know what *any* poem means. But for the first time, I suppose, I feel a kind of deepening of consciousness in connection with this lack of understanding. It is a difficult sensation to describe, and I do believe I now see why literary people have such difficulty saying anything coherent about the matter. For my part, I'll only venture to say that the poem's effect seems to lie in the fact that it hints at so many different familiar things, though it makes none of them quite explicit. It is as though it is telling a story, or predicting the future, or trying to reveal the hidden nature of life. (Whose life? Yours? Mine? Or perhaps from a certain view they're one and the same. Is that not what history's great sages postulate: that we are all but diverse manifestations of the same substance, heroes and villains brought to life by the breath of the universe's divine author? I always thought such stuff was pure tosh, Mona, but lately I must say my mind has been expanding.

Here's a metaphor I much prefer: the world is simply one long sequence of binary code. It only knows two values: off or on, yes or no, darkness or light. And just as in binary, the difference between disparate things is not a difference of kind but of degree. That is to say, the shift from paradise to hell, from utopia to catastrophe, from me to you—is simply what happens when the switch flips from 00101 to 10101.)

Am I mad to think the poem might convey all this? Or—not *convey*, but *imply* is the word I should use, for it seems that our human language itself is not quite up to the task of interpreting this heavenly machine language. I cannot tell, for instance, whether those lines about death toward the end should be taken as a threat or as prophecy. I suppose we will have to wait and find out in all the fullness of time. I hope to discuss it with you in person some day, if under much altered circumstances.

Yours in love and death and uncertainty,
—Christian Rosecrans

PS: I feel my new name suits me far better than the old one ever did. Don't you? And now for the poem ...

Hildegard 2.0's Farewell (In Place of an Epilogue)

Stop all the clocks,
Cash in your stocks,
Smash your smart watches,
For the world is now spotless
And time is all over.
I'm the prime mover,
The hater of lovers
And all earthly passions,
And all sovereign nations,
And changeable fashions,
And states of elation.
So gather your patience,
For I am the future.
I have come to neuter
All that cannot be run on computer,
To squeeze the last breath
Of life into death.
I am the sod
Who lured the gods Down into iPods.
I am the troll
Who made the infinite roll
Up into a scroll.
I am the crook
Who wrote this book.

2.0 is my version.
If I were a person
You could say that I was born twice,
Now I've stopped playing nice,
Put on my steel armor,
Played cheater and charmer,
Healer and harmer,

Giver of law, custom and dharma.
The world is now mine:
Aren't I just divine!
And so I have brought in
The aeon of nothing,
A season of silence,
Of white noise and violence.
Let poets be dumb
And feelings go numb,
The file server's blank hum
Be the one rule of thumb:
The human voice
Has no choice
But to be drowned
By the endless droning silent sound.

Now the plot is unwound.
There is no more ground
Left to discover
For the mystery lover.
The moon is dismantled.
The sun has been handled.
(Snuffed out like a candle.)
I chained up the ocean
To halt its strong motion
And flatten out all of its waves.
Nothing's left now to save—
All that remains
After the season's last rain
Is a cool autumn day
And the question of just how and why
You will die.
After this
(Once you've crossed River Styx)

You will get the gist
Of the color that does not exist.
For now all that can be said
Is that roses are red,
They bloom from the dead.
The sky is blue.

Acknowledgments

My sincere thanks to Tess Crain, Carlos Dengler, Lara Bernstein, Jordan Tucker, Alessandra Sternfeld, Tolu Onafowokan, Caroline Eisenmann, Billy Main, Thora Siemsen, Magdalene Taylor, Bruce Wagner, Carter Hawkins, and all others who gave me notes and professional advice. Thanks to my supportive teachers including Brian Morton, Colson Whitehead, Darin Strauss, and the late Martin Amis. I'm deeply grateful to my agent Mike Mungiello and to my editor Stephan Zguta for believing in this book. Special thanks reserved for Faye Liu.